MEDICINE WOMAN

FRANK KIDD

For my brothers, my first fans

CHAPTER 1
DEATH TREES

LEVI THURSTON WOKE WET, MISERABLE, AND in pain. It was the morning's dew that first woke him, having soaked through his buckskin pants and into his bones, but it was the arrow still lodged in his shoulder that brought him to full consciousness.

His breath rattled and he coughed into his hand. He searched the phlegm for blood, and finding none, sighed relief. The arrow had only pierced his shoulder, not a lung. A fortunate thing.

Then he ran his fingers over the jagged remains of the arrow's shaft, tensing against the pain. He'd broken it off last night, just after he'd made his run. Just after he'd lost his horse, having been stolen by the same Utes that had tagged him with the arrow.

Around him, the mountains were still. Too still, with only the faint whisper of the wind moving through the treetops and the sky just beginning to lighten.

And above him, a skeletal hand hung delicately off the side of the burial platform he'd apparently spent the night beneath. Finger bones held in place by little dried bits of gristle. He cringed at the sight and fumbled around for his rifle, letting out a sigh of relief as his hand closed around the smooth maple stock of the Hawken. Come what may, he still had his rifle.

He struggled to his feet then, ignoring the ache in his bum shoulder, and took stock of his surroundings.

He was in a small canyon of sorts, more platforms woven into the trees around him like so many floating tombs. Skeletons wrapped in blankets, some of them still wearing their beads and feathers. They stared at him from their floating beds, gaping eye sockets following his every move. Ragged ceremonial feathers shifting slightly in the small breeze, ghostlike, almost alive.

This was a bad place and he'd just spent the night in it. The realization didn't sit well with him.

He hadn't known where he was last night, dark as it was, but it explained why the Utes had given up the chase. Damned things buried their dead in trees and let the birds and buzzards pick them clean. Something about bringing their spirits closer to the sky.

They'd stolen his horse, and his mule, or rather he'd left them. Took off on foot as fast as he could when he caught the arrow. It had been just nigh of dark when they'd come upon him, and he kicked himself for not picking a better camp. But the Utes had always been friendly enough with him, even traded a time or two, and he hadn't seen any fresh sign for days. He'd let his guard down, and had paid the price.

And that was the thing with Injuns—you could never quite figure out what one was thinking or planning. At all times, a man had to be on the lookout.

There'd only been three of them, he figured. Probably, they were just young bucks looking to count coup and prove themselves, and not a proper war party. But there was no real telling.

He started off after that with the burial trees and their dead residents providing silent company. Then he followed a dry creek bed up into higher country, and finally found his way clear of the place.

LEVI PAUSED UNDER THE SHADE OF A cottonwood to scan the way he'd come. Nothing stirred.

He took stock of his weapons—he still had the Hawken which was chambered in .53, a horn of powder, and a bag of caps and balls. His hatchet and his scalper knife still hung on his belt. Everything else was with his horse, and by proxy the Utes, to include a brace of pistols and a smoothbore flintlock he kept loaded with buck and ball.

He wished he had those pistols now. The Hawken was the best, but when the fight got up close and personal, nothing beat having a pistol or two. If those braves came back looking for him, he'd get one good shot out of the Hawken, maybe two if they were a ways off, and then it would be hand to hand. And that smoothbore, loaded with both buck and ball, was no finer weapon to stop a charge, for he'd often cut down two or more Indians with a single shot.

Working diagonally up the mountain, he found a small spring and a place where the water pooled. He threw himself into the water in an attempt to wash off the stink of death. Though clear of the graveyard, he still felt dirty, as if death was communicable.

It was about midday when he found the cave, and the pain in his shoulder finally outweighed the urge to put distance between him and any potential pursuers. Less of a cave and more of an overhang, wider than it was deep, he figured that a fire in the back of it would be okay. The smoke would diffuse across the rock ceiling and travel upward, scattering along the face of the mountain. And he was so high up that any smell would be carried away on the high country winds and dissipate over miles.

As he inspected his shelter, he noticed the dead branches scattered about the back of it, in an unnatural sort of way, as if they'd once been gathered. He wondered at that, for if they were gathered, it had no doubt been by a man. But a long time ago by the looks of it. This country had a way of fooling a man into thinking he was the first to ever see it, but that wasn't ever really true.

He gathered the sticks together and piled on the leaf litter. Sparks caught the spoonful of powder he poured from his horn and a bright orange flame flashed to life. He added small twigs, nursing the flame to good health.

He sat there for a while, just warming his hands, dreading what he needed to do.

But when the fire was going hot, he set the blade of the scalper knife in the beginnings of its coals. Then, shrugging out of his shirt, and careful to guide the remains of the arrow through the hole where it had pierced his buckskin, he examined the wound.

He hoped to God they'd used a stone head. Some of the tribes had started to use iron arrowheads, cut from pig iron that they traded for. He'd seen a few men snatch such an arrow and the results were always ugly. They bent inside the body, or bunched up next to a bone, and made for a hell of a time getting them back out. Did more damage on the way out than in.

Taking the buckskin shirt, he used it to grip the arrow shaft, now slick with blood, and wrenched the arrow out. It came free in a blaze of white-hot pain and anger climbed his gut. Pain made him mad, and he sucked wind through his front teeth. But it felt good too. The same relief one got from plucking a splinter, and it came in equal proportion to the size of the splinter.

He felt consciousness fade, but he refused to go, refocusing on his breath. Breathing controlled the pain. Steadied the mind.

He refocused his attention on the arrow in hand. It was bloody and short. About four inches in all—with a stone head.

He slapped the hot blade over his wound and clenched his eyes shut, counting to ten in his head. He only made it to five before removing hot iron from flesh, so he slapped it back down and started the count over.

Such was his way of discipline. There was no room for weakness of the mind. The body was its own thing, wanting what it couldn't have. But he could allow none of it. He had to be in charge if he was to survive. Nothing could run him, not pain, nor fear.

With the full count complete, he removed the knife and collapsed backwards on the stone floor. He lay there panting and sweating for a long while. His vision narrowed. He found faces in the rock ceiling above him. Waves of heat and pain washed over him. Sweat beaded, burnt flesh nauseated.

And in those dim moments, where all was silent, and the walls of consciousness pushed in on him he wondered if he was to die alone. Here, in this cave where no one would know the better. The idea of it scared him.

He looked and smelled like an animal. His hair was dark brown, long and knotted, and his fist-length beard matched. At just over six feet tall, he was panther lean and bigger than most men. He had always been proud of his size, even though he'd not had a hand in it. It had made fighting easier, and getting on with women was never a problem, even though they mostly cared about the size of his purse—at least the kind of women he'd ever had access to. Yet here, lying on the cave floor, he felt small. Small and insignificant.

The moccasins he wore were Shoshone. His deerskin pants traded for off the Crow. Same as his fringed buckskin shirt. All of which, besides his weapons, now seemed the limits of his possessions.

His age lay somewhere past his twentieth birthday but not yet his thirtieth, he knew not which was closer for he'd lost track. He'd trapped, hunted, and fought the mountains for over a decade, and each year he made it further West. It was his fourteenth birthday when he ran off from his father's farm in the middle of the night. He called it a farm, but you could hardly call what they did in the Smoky Mountains farming. And he wondered then if the old bastard he'd called a father was still alive.

When the Company had set its eyes on the plains, he'd been one of the first to ride a keelboat up the Missouri, or at least second since Lewis and Clark. Which was not at all true, but made for big talk around a campfire.

But they were only stories. That was the sum of him. Stories about silent places that no one would remember, about a life that no one would mourn. It had always been a lonely life, of that, he was sure. He'd thought often of taking a wife, but the opportunity never came, and if it did he doubted he could stay in one place. This was the measure of him. The measure of a man who ended up cornered and dying in a dirty cave, dying like some wounded animal, and no further along than the earliest of his forebears.

Then sleep—or unconsciousness—found him.

CHAPTER 2
RETRIBUTION

THE FIRE HAD BURNED DOWN TO NOTHING but a pile of embers. Levi stood up and kicked what remained of the coals, then walked to the edge of the cave in a crouch, scanning his surroundings.

It was morning. He'd slept the whole rest of the day yesterday, and all night. His muscles were stiff, and his shoulder flamed, but he ignored it.

The birds chirped below him, and he craned his ears for any sounds out of place: a rock accidentally sent tumbling down the mountain, the snap of a twig, the dull click of hooves against stone, or even the chatter of squirrels sounding an alarm. But he heard nothing. Nothing but the busy, stillness of the mountain. The quiet loudness of nature.

Levi shrugged back into his shirt. Gathered up the Hawken. And set foot towards lower country. He had to stay moving on the off chance his fire had given him away. Moreover, he needed to find a mount if he was to survive. A man without a horse had slim chance to none in this country. But more specifically, he wanted *his* horse and *his* mule back.

It was the horse he missed. He'd taken a right

liking to the horse. She was a painted Comanche pony, red with white splotches, and had a lopsided splash of white over her right eye. The Comanche bred the finest horseflesh this side of the Mississippi. In fact, they were the only tribe that bred their own horses. The others simply preferred to steal them. But the Comanche knew horses, and they knew the secrets of good blood, and that little paint knew both the mountains and the plains. She was a runner too, run herself to death for him if he let her. And a fighter. She'd bite a man if he got too close.

He'd named her Sheba, like in the Bible, mostly on account of how beautiful he found her, and on account of how she'd come to him—he stole her.

The pain in his shoulder faded as he made his way back down the other side of the slope. He wasn't especially keen on picking a fight with the Utes while he had a bad shoulder, but he also wasn't too keen on walking everywhere. Besides, he owed them a fight.

Levi had never been in the habit of letting a man steal from him, and he wasn't about to start now. He'd seen it before. A man let this or that slide for long enough and the world would rob him blind. He'd grown up biblical ways, but out here it was an eye for an eye. Forgiveness was for places with laws. No, if you stole from him, you could count on having to give it back, and the interest he charged wasn't usually worth the price of the loan.

It was nigh evening, and the sun was ticking lower in the sky when he found the place for his ambush. It was on the edge of a small meadow that dropped off into a small timbered ravine.

He dragged wood up and stacked it high. Then gathered brush from the trees and lit it off. About the same time that the sun clicked below the horizon, the fire he built was ablaze. He'd built it awful big and it still strained his imagination that Injuns thought a man so stupid.

If they were still in the pass looking for him, they'd be on him in no time. It wasn't the first time he'd built a fire to lure in some braves. He'd always wondered whether they suspected a trap or not. They never seemed to. Sneaking right up on the fire, with no mind to the darkness beside them.

He'd heard folks say Indians were stupid, but that was a lie. They were anything but. They were as clever as any white man, maybe twice as much when it came to the wild places. More pragmatic too. However, that sort of thing cut both ways, and he had found that it was a reciprocal lack of respect that seemed to most often do them in. That was the only thing that explained it. They saw a fire, knew a white man was about, and they just assumed that he was a tenderfoot.

The fire blazed, and Levi slipped off into the darkness. He picked a likely spot on the edge of the ravine, figuring the way they'd come, having built the blazing campfire in such a way that there were only a few likely points of approach.

An hour passed slowly, then another, and at last he heard a horse snort some ways off.

They were here. Maybe already on him.

As if on cue, a shadow passed beneath him, then another. They moved softly, barely making a noise, quieter than ghosts. His heart thrummed as the short hairs on his neck stood on end.

When they had passed by, he moved backwards through the dark, picking his way slowly and quietly in the direction he'd heard the horse snort. He'd find the third man there.

At the bottom of the ravine, he caught the movements of horses. He crept up on them, eyes wide, straining against the black of night. He paused and crouched. His ears strained—the small munching of grass, the shifting of the horses, their gentle breathing.

And their smell comforted him, the dusty, musky smell of hard worked horses. It was a smell that a man would not normally consider pleasant, but he'd come to associate it with his world being in an upright enough place. And if you could smell a horse, it meant you had one, and if you had a horse, you had a fighting chance.

The breeze was in his face, likely why they hadn't gone spooky on him. He moved closer, until he was no less than ten yards away from the grazing shadows. He drew his knife and set the Hawken gently against a tree, taking a mental note of exactly where he left it, and the exact number of steps back to it.

He still hadn't spotted the last Indian, the one they'd no doubt left behind to guard the horses.

He felt around on the ground by his feet and plucked a small stone up from the earth. Then he threw it a little way away in the opposite direction. The stone bounced through leaves. The horses snorted, one threw his head up in alert. Still, his human quarry didn't stir, so he waited.

It seemed an eternity had passed between the sound of the stone, and the appearance of the figure. Then a human shape emerged from the shadows behind the horses and looked off in the direction of the sound.

Levi made his move then, covering the distance to the brave on the padded balls of his feet. The Ute turned to meet him but was too late. Levi had a hold on him from behind, his great hand clamped over the man's mouth, wrenching his neck backwards even as his knife plunged upwards beneath his ribs.

The Indian bucked forward, trying to shake him, and then heaved himself backwards slamming both of them to the ground. He was smaller than Levi, by quite a lot, but all muscle and sinew, and it took everything in him to keep the little man's back.

Levi pulled the knife from its place in the man's side and plunged again, this time finding the heart, and felt him shudder.

He rolled him off, pivoted to a knee, and took a handle on the dead man's hair by wrapping it around his hand. Then Levi took the knife and in a single swift, circular motion sliced the front of the man's hairline, snapping the scalp off with one forceful flick.

He'd seen others scalp a man by planting a foot on his face. This was an unnecessary step in his opinion, and somewhat uncouth. The way Levi did it was the way a Crows had once shown him. Just slice and then snap. There wasn't much to it, and no need to make a big show of it. Nor to be disrespectful by stepping on a man's face.

Levi threaded the scalp through his belt and checked the horses. Sheba nudged him and blew forcefully.

"Good girl," Levi said softly.

He gave the horse a pat, and slipped quietly back through the darkness to the place where he'd left the Hawken. The others would be back shortly. No doubt, they'd already figured the fire for a ruse.

He crouched in a pair of shadows cast by a big, crooked tree. It was dark beneath the trees, almost pitch black on account of no moon. He pulled the set trigger on the Hawken back with a click, and shifted his finger towards the front trigger, careful not to bump it, for once set, it was a hair trigger.

He heard movement behind him. They were coming. They had either heard his scuffle or smelled a trap; either way, they would know something was up.

The two braves stopped short, just forms moving about in the black of night. Then he heard a short, small gasp from one, and he knew they'd found their friend.

Levi pointed the rifle and a twig snapped beneath him.

He pulled the trigger.

The flash from the barrel of his rifle blinded him. He heard the thwap of his bullet finding the near shadow's flesh, and then instinctively he threw the Hawken up in a blocking motion. This move, borne of both instinct and experience, likely saved his life, for the rifle's stock met the downward swing of the second brave's club with a crack.

And then they were on top of each other. Rolling around in the dark, looking for a grip on the other—a tangled mass of limbs. Levi caught a wrist, and when the Indian tried to roll away, he felt resistance. He torqued the wrist in the direction of the resistance until he heard a loud pop and then a snap, and the brave screamed in agony.

Levi rolled to his feet as the Indian scrambled for the horses, which had since spooked and were snorting and stomping behind them.

Levi snapped the tomahawk up from his belt and tackled the man to the ground, catching ahold of his leg first, and then pawing himself forward onto the man's back. Atop the man, now pinned to the ground, he dispatched him with a single blow to the back of the head.

Then slowly it quieted. And he slumped backwards, his breath ragged, and his bad shoulder totally inflamed.

He reloaded the Hawken next, his hands shaking

as the war spirit left his body. He relieved the two other braves of their hair, clipped their scalps onto his belt, and mounted Sheba. His mule was there too, still loaded down the way he'd left him.

He'd named the mule Jackwagon on account of him being a pain in his ass most days. And he took the brave's horses, three fine Indian ponies, that he could trade off to the Shoshone, the root-diggers, or maybe even the Crow.

CHAPTER 3
LOKI

LEVI STOPPED FOR THE MORNING BY THE banks of a river. He slid off the back of Sheba and kneeled at the water's edge before filling his water-skin. As he did so, the hairs on the back of his neck pricked and a chill ran through his body. Not from anything he'd heard, or smelled, but from something he'd sensed.

He'd long held that man had a sixth sense, some latent ability that lay untapped when hidden behind Fort walls or living in towns or cities. It was a prey sense. Deer had it too. That moment when the aether tells them something's not quite right, or that they are being watched or stalked—hunted. Half the time when he was hunting, he looked out past the animal, and never directly at it, out of an occult respect for this mysterious sense. But he'd learned to trust it too.

He eased his hand towards one of the percussion pistols in his belt, and then whirled, pulling the piece at the same instant he turned.

An old man, an Indian, sitting deathly still on a

rock no more than ten feet behind him just stared at him.

Levi hadn't seen him when he rode up, and he struggled to believe that he'd missed him, and he struggled even more to believe the old man had just snuck up and sat down.

"The hell you come from old man," Levi called.

The old man grinned. Yellow and missing teeth. His clothes looked Lakota, which was odd because he was a bit south of their normal range.

The old man said something in his native tongue. Levi didn't understand it. But he picked out a few words, like "bad," and "medicine." He could speak Crow, which was similar to Lakota, but akin to translating Italian to Spanish in its usefulness.

Levi responded with hands outstretched. Then he signed to the old man, "What do you want?" He saw a spark of recognition in the old man's eye. He'd understood. Sign language was universal on the plains. Every tribe knew it. It was a course and pragmatic language where big ideas could be transmitted for the purposes of trade or war, but all nuance was lost.

"You slept in bad place," the old man signed. "Very bad medicine."

"No choice. Utes behind me," Levi responded. The old man was of course talking about his night in the boneyard.

"Curse very bad," the old man signed.

"I don't need medicine," Levi signed. "No bad."

The old man looked somber and shook his head.

"I come." The old man motioned, pointing first at himself and then at Levi.

"I go North," Levi said. "But you can't come."

"Big warrior," the old man pointed at the scalps hanging on Levi's belt. "I am warrior too," he signed.

"I'm not looking for help," Levi responded.

"I come," the old man signed.

Levi ignored him. He'd ridden with others often enough, even an Indian a time or two, but he was trying to get north and start trapping, and he wanted to be settled by the first snow. He had a little cabin up there that he'd hidden away right on the northern edge of the Wind River range. He'd winter there, and he'd like to be well settled before the first snow. It was late summer now, and the leaves were mighty close to changing.

He mounted Sheba and pulled the mule up alongside him, then he nodded goodbye to the old man and left him sitting alone on his little rock. The old man didn't move.

MOUNTAINS ROSE ON EITHER SIDE OF HIM, peaks pierced the sky. Mountain goats played with one another a long way up and looked like little white dots of paint flecked artfully on God's canvas. At one point, he saw a Moose on the other side of the river, but it just watched him pass, not paying too much mind to him.

He was in the saddle for the better part of two hours, just following the river north, when Sheba laid her ears back. Levi twisted in the saddle, the Hawken laid out over his lap, and tried to spot what had spooked her. He hadn't seen no Indian sign, and it'd been awful peaceful, so it figured he'd run into something. The Indian ponies he led along behind him sensed it too, for they snorted and flicked their ears.

The coyote came running up to them then, leaving its hiding place in the trees to playfully dance across the open space between them. Sheba started to bolt, but she settled down at Levi's gentle command. She'd never quite taken to Loki, and only tolerated his occasional presence because she trusted Levi. The Indian ponies were spooked, but didn't try to run.

Levi drew the horses to a halt and dug around for a bit of jerky in his pack, then tossed it to the lone coyote, which had danced himself right up to them. He watched as the wild dog scarfed the meat, not bothering to inspect it first. Then Levi nudged Sheba forward and Loki walked alongside.

Levi had found him as a pup. Never knew how he got separated from his momma, and never found his den either. Found him just after a lightning storm, when he was all wet and trembling underneath a little rock overhang. He had growled at Levi, cute little snarls, that had somehow made him seem all the more pathetic at the time. Levi coaxed him out of his little wet hidey hole with a bit of meat and snatched him up with a buffalo robe.

It had started as a thing to do. Levi, having heard tell that coyotes could be tamed, same as any dog, if you caught them as a pup, figured he'd put it to the test. He'd known a fellow back in the Smokey's whose daughter had a whole passel of critters, raccoons and badgers and such, that ate right out of her hand. She was right homely looking though, and he'd often wondered how much trouble finding a husband it had caused her. The critters, not the homeliness.

He'd let the pup tag along, tending to it and feeding it. Named it Loki, after the Norse trickster. His father had been some mix of Irish and Scottish, and a storyteller when he wasn't raging drunk. He'd occasionally told him the old stories he'd been told when he himself was nothing but a pup. Their line could be traced back to the Danish raiders he'd say. How he could know this for certain, Levi never knew, but he supposed there was truth to it for he knew the stories.

He'd told him about Thor and his brother Loki, and Yggdrasil the world tree, and Odin their father. So, he'd named the pup Loki, after the trickster, and figured it a fitting enough name.

Loki would often raise his hackles and growl friendly like at his touch, but never really took to tagging along the way a dog did and had very little ability to follow commands. He was still a wild creature, and as such, came and went as he pleased. But he was not without his uses.

He'd appeared often enough, with a yip or a yelp, to alert Levi that someone or something was trailing him. He'd even occasionally been woken in the middle of the night by the Coyote's screams, just in time to find a brave or two trying to count coup or steal his horse. He would go weeks without seeing the animal, and then be paid a visit when he least expected it. And he often wondered how closely the dog shadowed him.

Nearest he could figure it, Loki thought him family. Coyotes didn't really live and hunt in packs the same way wolves did. They usually lived semi-separate, but in the same territory-like. Helping the others in the family group out when they could, alerting each other to food and danger.

Levi watched the Coyote lope alongside them. It had been two weeks since he'd last seen him. His fur was short and golden, and he'd grown large. Maybe on account of all the scraps Levi had fed him, or perhaps he had a bit of wolf somewhere in his near lineage.

In any case, he was glad the dog was alright, and happy to have his company.

He hit a lope as he guided Sheba back towards the

trees, mostly to try and get out of the sun, when she stumbled quite suddenly.

As she tumbled, Levi threw himself clear of her, and rolled up to his knees. He had the Hawken up to his shoulder and scanned the edge of the clearing looking for more Utes, as he figured Sheba had just taken an arrow. But there was no sound, no war whoop, no sign of Indians.

Loki stood a way off just looking at him, but besides the commotion, didn't seem alarmed. The mule had already lit out for the trees, bucking furiously in an attempt to free himself of his pack.

The Indian ponies had ran in the opposite direction.

Sheba snorted, still on her side. She attempted to get back up to her feet, then collapsed back onto her side. Levi picked himself up slowly, his heart in his throat.

She'd broken her leg in a gopher hole.

He knelt beside her, putting pressure on her shoulder so she didn't try to get up again.

"Easy girl," he said.

She blew forcefully, her nostrils flared, body trembling. She was breathing fast, in quick short gasps, on account of the pain. She tried to move, whinnied, then collapsed once more. Levi steeled himself, and tried to quiet the sadness in his gut.

He pulled a pistol. And then thought better of it.

Firing off a gun could just bring more unwanted guests down on him.

He replaced the pistol and pulled his knife.

Pet the quivering horse.

"Damn you, ol' girl. Where am I going to find another one like you."

Levi ground his teeth and flexed his hands, letting

the anger and the hurt boil. He'd just gotten her back, dammit.

Then with a single hard swipe of the blade he freed her of the pain, and almost immediately wished he'd taken his chances with the pistol.

He wiped the blood on his hands off on the meadow grass next to him, and then collapsed backwards, leaning against her lifeless body.

Loki curled up a few feet away from him, and they both sat there for a long while.

He thought about the gopher hole, and how she'd broke her leg clean in two, the stupid horse. No Indians had attacked. He hadn't been running her hard. He hadn't even seen it, and obviously she hadn't. It was an accident, a freak accident.

He thought then about chance. Freak chance. And curses. And the part of him that wasn't normally superstitious thought about the old mountain folk tales about curses and witchcraft and such. The part of him that believed in snake charmers and faith healing, and little wicker nests hung to keep the devil away, all this had happened because he disturbed the dead. Levi tried to ignore the thought, but the Old Indian's warning had already burrowed deep into the base of his neck, and it hung there as a dead weight, heavy as a millstone.

"You were born under a dark star son," his father used to say. And for a small second, Levi was eleven years old again, and his father, blind-drunk, drool in his red beard, was slumped in a planter's chair, explaining to him through slurred speech how he was the reason that he drank, and how he'd drank every day since Levi was born, since he'd killed his own mother coming out of her womb. "It was under a blood moon, boy. I knew as soon as she started, it would end badly," he'd said.

It seemed bad medicine ran in the family. Levi patted Sheba, her body already growing cold. "I'm sorry ol' girl."

LOKI'S EARS PERKED FIRST, THEN HE GAVE A low growl, which came out more like a protective snarl. "Quiet boy," Levi said. A figure appeared at the edge of the meadow, the wild flowers coming up to his waist, and the rest of him still in shadow. Levi cocked a pistol, but did not move from his seat.

Then the figure came walking towards them, bringing Jackwagon along behind. How he'd caught that mule, he'd never know, but it was the old Indian.

Old Man stopped in front of them, and Loki didn't stop growling. The Indian eyed the coyote warily, yet curiously.

Old Man motioned at Sheba, and signed, "bad medicine."

"Quiet Loki," Levi said, and the coyote kept snarling.

"You are friends with Coyote?" the old man signed, pointing at the dog. He looked confused and a bit fearful.

Loki snarled again and gave a small lunge.

"Oh, get on, git." Levi said. "He's not doing nothing."

The coyote ran off a ways then, circling once, before disappearing into the trees.

Levi pushed himself up to his feet and snatched the mule's lead from the old man. Then pulled his saddle free of Sheba. He'd be on foot for the foreseeable future. It was that or stash some of the shit Jackwagon was carrying. The mule couldn't carry both his things and him.

"A powerful healer in the Blackfoot tribe," the old man signed.

"I ain't cursed," Levi said.

"She can remove bad medicine."

Levi pulled Jackwagon forward, towards the trees. The old man followed behind him.

Levi had seen horses go down, seen broken legs before, but what he had trouble believing was that it could happen to Sheba. That animal was so sure-footed. She was mountain bred, had mustang in her. Of all the horses for some shit like that to happen to, Sheba would have been the last. They continued up the trail in silence, the Old Indian following along behind.

THEY CAMPED COLD THAT NIGHT, HUDDLED up beneath a little rock crevice that sheltered them from the wind. Old Man didn't complain. Levi pulled a big Buffalo coat from the back of the mule and curled up inside of it. It was still summer, but it got cold at night, high up as they were.

The stars winked and spun overhead, and Levi watched them as they did. The old man sat board straight, back against a rock, and stared out at the night. Levi didn't remember when he drifted off, but he did, and when he woke again it was in the middle of the night having to piss.

The stars had shifted. Old Man was still sitting but his eyes were closed, and he seemed asleep.

Levi shrugged out of the buffalo robe, pulled himself to his feet, and then wandered off a little way down the trail to relieve himself.

He had just finished when he heard it.

A low whistle, just like the kind that a human

makes. Made his blood run cold, and he knew it wasn't a bird, cus he'd spent many years in the wild places and never heard a whistle like that. Especially at night.

He cinched up his pants in a hurry and buckled his belt, doing double-time back to the rock crevice. The whistle came again from somewhere behind him, but this time closer.

Levi felt two competing urges. One telling him to answer back, and the other telling him to run fast as he could until he was completely clear of this God forsaken country.

He hurried back to the sleeping place, and as he approached he spotted the old man. Now wide awake and alert. He sat board straight, his eyes peeled wide.

Levi started to whisper something to the old man, but the old man shot him a look so harsh that it stopped him dead. The old Indian raised a single finger to his lips, and shook his head no.

Levi eased himself down, and they both sat there in silence for the remainder of the night. Just staring out at the darkness.

The whistle did not happen again, but neither did sleep.

Dawn broke and they packed quickly and quietly, then set a pace down the mountain. When they were some ways clear of the place, and the sun was fully above them, Levi found courage enough to speak.

"What was that?"

"Evil spirit," the Old Man replied.

"They whistle?" Levi signed back. The whole thing seemed silly now under the sun's golden rays.

The Old Man signed something about spirits and hunting.

"That's a sinister thing to say," Levi said, not bothering to sign.

"The dead follow you," the Old Man signed again, then shrugged his shoulders as if saying I told you so.

They walked on, and the land changed from brown to green, then to a deep red, and the mountains became less mountains and more towers, tall rock spires with rusty hue.

About midday, Jackwagon refused to take a step further.

Levi let the mule graze, while he and the old man retreated to the shade of a nearby tree.

"This medicine woman?" Levi asked. "She can get rid of the curse? Chase off the evil spirits." All day on foot had started to work on him. He said he didn't believe in magic, or curses, or the like, but what man didn't? And was there anything that could explain such a run of bad luck? Out here, a man was alone. All he had was his wits and luck. And if he didn't have any luck, how long before he ended up dead?

"Maybe," the old man said.

"How far away is she?" Levi asked.

"Far," the old man signed. "We would need horses."

"I don't need you along," Levi said.

The old man shrugged and said something in his own language.

"And you're sure this medicine woman can help?" Levi asked once more.

"Very powerful," the old man signed. "Many tribes scared of Blackfoot right now."

The Blackfoot roamed just above the Medicine Bow, just past his cabin maybe a few weeks ride. He could go, see this lady luck, this young Medicine Woman. She could fix his curse and he could make it back to the cabin before winter came. But it was a fool's errand, for the Blackfoot hated whites, or most at least, and they were a fearsome race, preferring scalps and war honors to trade.

"And how come you want to go?" Levi asked.

The Old Man's face darkened for a second, and he said nothing, but then he smiled again; that old wise smile that had already started to irritate Levi.

"Friends. Want to see, one last time," he said.

Levi said nothing more, but already a plan had started to form in his mind.

They walked down the canyon in silence then, and at the bottom of it found the Indian ponies that had ran off. They were grazing peacefully.

"It's a good sign," the old man said. "You made the right decision."

"I never said I was going to go see that Blackfoot healer," Levi said.

The old Indian shrugged.

"But it looks like I got to now," Levi said slowly.

CHAPTER 4
THE MEDICINE WOMAN

APANIAKI WALKED TO THE RIVER, THE bundle of water gourds dangling at her side. Birds chirped above her, and the summer grass smelled sweet. A butterfly, her namesake, landed on a patch of Lupine just up the rocky trail ahead of her. Its brilliant orange wings setting fire to the wildflower's purples and greens.

She heard movement. A blur of tanned flesh and buckskin grabbed her by the shoulders and shattered her silence. Strong arms and an iron grip spun her around. It was Large Teeth or He-Has-Large-Teeth.

She shoved him off her, and he danced backwards playfully.

"So unaware," Large Teeth said. He was smiling, but he didn't really have large teeth as his name suggested. If he had, he'd certainly grown into them, Apaniaki thought. He was handsome by all accounts, and the top of her father's list for potential husbands. High cheekbones, a strong jaw framed by long, black hair. But he was also arrogant, and had a cruel streak that scared her.

She turned back towards the river, ignoring him.

She had decided long ago that a studied disinterest in any suitors was the clearest path to avoiding a broken heart. Her father would make the decision, and she would live with it.

"What's wrong?" Large Teeth said. He followed behind her.

"I don't want to talk," Apaniaki replied.

"It was a long hunt," Large Teeth said. "I killed many Black Horn and made gifts of the robes to your father."

Apaniaki knelt at the river's edge and began filling the gourds with water. "You shouldn't be out here," Apaniaki said. "Others will tell stories."

"Let them talk," Large Teeth said.

"You would like that," Apaniaki said. "Many women makes you a big man."

"We will go raiding soon," Large Teeth said, ignoring her. "It will be my first of the Horse Raids. I will steal Buffalo Runners. I will make more gifts to your father."

"You better hurry then. Spotted Locust talks of the same," Apaniaki replied. She watched his brow furrow, and his eyes flash with jealousy.

For only a moment, she felt a tinge of guilt for throwing it so callously in his face. If he wasn't so forceful, so forward, he would find her more willing to indulge the thought of him. But as it stood, the thought of tending his lodge, and bearing his children turned her stomach.

A rider came up the trail. He was pushing the horse fast. When he cleared the trees further up, Apaniaki recognized him. It was Gray Wolf. He drew the horse up in front of them, the animal snorted and pranced, the wind at his feet and fire in his belly.

"We have wounded," Gray Wolf said, holding out his arm to her.

She ran to him then, and grabbed his outstretched arm as he pulled her up onto the back of the horse behind him in one swift motion.

SEVERAL WARRIORS STOOD OUTSIDE RED Beaver's lodge. Their faces painted red, torsos smattered with ash and blood, their deerskin pants caked with mud.

Red Beaver flung the leather flap of the lodge open, and waved her in. He was old now and gray like an old silver bear. His shoulders slumped from the weight of several moons, but his eyes remained young and playful, seeing everything, perceiving more. He was both healer and sage, and she had learned all he had to teach.

She entered silently.

A brave lay on his back in the center of the teepee, half covered with a thick buffalo robe. He was sweating profusely, obviously taken by great evil.

Red Beaver drew the thick buffalo robe back to reveal a large, ragged hole in the man's flesh. He was still bleeding despite the strips of rawhide shoved into the wound.

"They are Kainai," Red Beaver said. "They made war on the Long Knives and the Crow, take many scalps. Only he was wounded."

Apaniaki looked down at the man. His face was painted red, which was the way of the Blood Tribe. The Kainai were her cousins, cousins of the Piikani, just as the Siksika were cousins of the Piikani. Though the tribes were separate they had often come together in times of war.

Red Beaver put pressure on the wound.

"Moss, and clay?" Apaniaki asked.

"And powdered Heuchera to stop the bleeding." Red Beaver ordered.

Apaniaki handed him a small leather pouch from her medicine bag where she kept the powdered root. Then she slipped out of the teepee and ran off towards the river.

Clay was plentiful by the river, as most wet areas were reasonable places to look. But she had found a deposit of white clay there only a few days earlier, which was especially good for healing. It was set back from the riverbank where the gentle plain flooded in the springtime and remained dry the rest of the year.

She had made it a habit to memorize where she'd last seen different useful plants and items at each new place they stopped. Such was the reason for her long walks about the area. At each new place, Apaniaki would spend weeks exploring. The earth scattered its gifts across its face, and to receive them was but a matter of searching, and on occasion, asking.

Red Beaver had taught her much of what she knew. He had trained her in the different uses of the sacred plants and taught her where to look for them. He'd taught her how to stop bleeding, how to set a bone, the cures for swollen testicles, how to break a fever, and often how to rid one of evil spirits.

On the way to the river, she took a detour down a narrow ravine where she'd seen elderberries growing just a few days before. The thicket of berries was tall, and the area smelled sickly sweet from the rotting fruit that had fallen overripe off the vine. But there were still plenty there. She picked a few handfuls of the purplish black fruit, the kind that were just turning ripe. She would use these for a poultice. She paused and tossed a few in her mouth before continuing for the clay.

The moss she found in large clumps, growing in

the crevices of the rough limestone ledges that overlooked the river. Her memory was sharp, well trained from exercises in gathering, but also from learning the histories of her people.

Since she was a child, her mother had taught her the sacred stories. She had learned all of them by heart, centuries worth of happenings, and despite all of this, her mind never felt heavy, or overfull. In fact, quite the opposite, she saw the world with clear eyes. A world perfectly ordered, a world full of secrets, but its magic made knowable. She spoke the language of the earth. The language of the plants, and the animals, and the trees. The language of the Thunder Maker, or the Heat Maker, and the language of Cold Maker.

WHEN APANIAKI RETURNED TO THE LODGE, it had just begun to grow dark. The brave was still alive, and the powdered Heuchera had helped stem the bleeding. She handed Red Beaver a wooden bowl with several lumps of white clay, and his eyes seemed to sparkle at the sight of it.

"Where did you get this?" he asked.

"By the river," Apaniaki replied. "I found it a few days ago."

"In all the times that we've camped here, I have never found white clay," the old man said proudly.

"Maybe its new, wise one," Apaniaki said.

The old man smiled. "Maybe it is."

She kneaded the elderberries to a pulp then and heated the mass over the fire outside the lodge. When the poultice of moss and elderberries was ready, she helped Red Beaver apply it. They then sealed over both the wound and the poultice with the white clay.

When they had finished, Apaniaki asked, "Do you think he will make it?"

"It is up to him now," Red Beaver said. "Him and his animal helper."

Apaniaki nodded.

"Go, get some sleep little one," Red Beaver said. "I am old, and do not sleep. I will stay with him."

Apaniaki smiled and hugged Red Beaver good night.

The next morning, before the sun had fully risen, Apaniaki made her way back to Red Beaver's teepee. He sat outside, wrapped in a buffalo robe, by the glowing coals of his fire. He was watching the sunrise, and when he saw Apaniaki, he smiled. But she knew him too well, for it was a tired smile, and a sad smile.

"He didn't make it?" she asked.

"It was his time," Red Beaver said matter of factly.

"You should have sent for me," Apaniaki said.

"And what would you have done little one, what would you have done that the spirits could not?" Red Beaver asked. "It is alright. It is not our choice."

Apaniaki sat beside the old man then and stared into the red glowing coals of the fire. Tears fell from her eyes, and she grieved for the young brave within, even though she did not know him.

It was then that Shining Feathers came passing by, already up and gathering water for the morning. She stopped in front of them, back bent under the weight of age. Her hair was silver, and she had a jagged hole where her nose had been taken from her. She was a Cut-Nose, a once unfaithful wife. She stopped, and upon seeing Apaniaki's tears, told her not to shed them, for if she shed them all now, she would not have any left, and she would surely need them.

Red Beaver threw a stone at the old woman and told her to leave.

"A Chief's daughter should know better," the grizzled woman scolded.

"Leave us," Red Beaver commanded.

The woman hissed softly and trudged on, the gourds of water sloshing and splashing as she carried them.

"What did she mean I will surely need them?" Apaniaki asked.

"She is old and bitter because her beauty was taken away," Red Beaver responded. "But her life is her own. Not all have clear sight."

Shining Feathers had always scared Apaniaki. She had often hid from her as a small child, for her face and missing nose had scared her. She remembered once, with much shame now, how she had thrown rocks at the woman and called her names with the other children. But she had not understood then.

The old woman was once young and beautiful, and had fallen in love with a young brave, or so the story went. But when it was time to marry, her father married her off to He-Who-Shouts, who had already married her older sister. This was common of course, for it was known that marrying sisters created a more harmonious lodge.

But Shining Feathers still loved the young brave, and so in secrecy, still met him. When she was found out, Gray Wolf, as was his right, beat her and took her beauty as was the merciful way to deal with unfaithful wives. After that, her lover would no longer talk to her. He died sometime later during a Black Horn hunt.

Apaniaki watched the old woman trudge off, one

of her feet dragging so that she left a trail in the dirt and leaves like a slug.

Apaniaki's heart broke for the old woman.

"Why did she say the daughter of a Chief should know better?" Apaniaki asked, as she choked back tears.

"She is bitter. No more," Red Beaver said. But his eyes betrayed him, and Apaniaki knew the reason.

As the daughter of the Chief, she would be married for honor, and taken for many gifts. Apaniaki had always known this, and so she hid herself. Hid herself from ever looking on a brave smile, or a loud confident voice with anything but cool apathy. She hid her heart lest anyone find it. What did not exist, could not be taken, or given—or broken.

APANIAKI THOUGHT OFTEN OF THE BRAVE that had died. She was well acquainted with death and had perhaps seen more than her fair share of it for one so young. Yet that brave visited her at night. He invaded her thoughts during the day. At an early age, she had realized that all things must come to an end, just as the seasons passed, so did the phases of life.

But it had never struck her just how precious it all was. Or how tragic when one so young was cut down at the height of it. The young warrior had fought bravely, but in Red Beaver's lodge she had seen fear in his eyes, a fear to go. What a mercy it would have been for him to die in battle, overcome by the spirits of war, and freely giving up his life.

It was evening, when the sun was still golden, and the squirrels played fitfully down the hill where her father found her. She was picking chokecherries and listening to the sounds of the river behind her. He came walking up the trail, his beautiful buckskins decorated with red and blue porcupine quills. He was Black Crow, but to her he was simply father.

She smiled halfheartedly at his approach and felt bad for avoiding him. She had thought, foolishly perhaps, that staying out of his sight would put her out of his mind. Where no doubt Spotted Locust and Large Teeth had kept her ever present.

Her father sat down on the limestone ledge beside her.

"You aren't so little anymore," her father said.

Apaniaki laughed softly, even as her heart dropped.

"I have made my decision," Black Crow said.

She stopped picking. She refused to look at him, choosing instead to stare at her berry-stained fingers.

"It is not so bad," Black Crow said. "You have many good suitors." He paused, waiting, but she gave no answer. "Don't you want to know who?"

The truth was that she didn't. Knowing would hardly make it better, somehow not knowing made it seem all the less real. She tried to respond to him but the lump in her throat precluded speaking, instead she sat there numbly.

"You know the story of when I found you," Black Crow said suddenly. "I have told you many times, but there is much you have not heard."

Apaniaki looked up. She had of course heard the story.

"Before I married Fox Kitten Woman, I was married to Singing Woman. She was my sits-besides-me wife. Things were good then and I kept her very warm at night. I hunted and raided often and had made a name for myself. I killed many Black Horn and took many scalps.

"We were happy. When she was with child we were overjoyed. My first child. I wanted a son. I told Singing Woman that she would give me many sons and she always laughed and told me that I would only have daughters.

"I sat outside the lodge as the old woman helped her. Singing Woman screamed loudly, and after each time, I strained my ears for any sound of my son.

"But then the Singing Woman stopped screaming, and no more sounds came from the tent. There was no little voice. There was no sound of Singing Woman. And then the Old Woman came to me, and she did not say anything, but I could see in her face that a great evil had occurred. They had both died.

"In my grief, I took to the hills, and cut my hair," Black Crow said. "I cut my arms with rocks and prayed for a vision at the top of the mountain."

Black Crow turned over his arms and Apaniaki saw the thick jagged scars that ran crossways. She'd always thought he'd taken them in battle. She'd never known it was grief that had been his enemy.

"I spent many days alone and no vision came," Black Crow continued. "I grew very angry, and I went looking for a fight. I had decided that I would die in battle. I would make war on whoever I found first.

"I found a camp of the Mandan, who traded with the Long Knives in those days. I prepared myself for war. I painted my face in the way that the Bear showed me, and I performed the sacred rites of my medicine bundle. I was prepared to take many scalps that day.

"But when I neared the camp, nothing stirred. It was quiet, very quiet. And a strange feeling came over me, as if death watched me from the trees. The Mandan camp seemed abandoned. Horses were still there, and dogs roamed the camp, but nobody else.

"I thought about leaving but I was too curious. The smell from the camp was terrible, and when I went into the lodges, I found many bodies. They were covered in flies, and bloated, and some already devoured by worms. They had been sick with the evil white scabs.

"Then I heard tiny cries—your tiny cries. They came from a lodge at the very edge of the camp.

"I hurried to the place and found you. Wrapped in a buffalo robe, I found you. You were a beautiful baby girl with eyes like the moon. I thought surely this was a gift. I thought that the Great One had heard my cries and brought me to my child. So, I picked you up and stole you away. With death all around me I had found the flame of life. I named you butterfly girl, for it was the first thing I saw when I left the camp."

Black Crow stopped his story then, tears brimming in his eyes, and Apaniaki hugged him. Then he held her at arm's length so he could look into her eyes.

"I knew you had strong medicine to survive when all around you was death. Now it is time for me to give you to another. Someday, I will die in battle, or on a hunt. You must have another to look after you. To protect you. Another who will keep you warm, and to have children of your own."

Apaniaki buried her head in his chest just as she had done when she was a little girl. She gripped him tightly and knew what he said was true.

"I have chosen Spotted Locust," he said.

"When?" Apaniaki asked simply, her voice cracking.

"Gray Wolf has located a herd of Black Horn," Black Crow said. "We will move camp. And then hold the union before the Black Horn hunt."

Apaniaki remained silent.

CHAPTER 5
ON CURSES

THE ROCKY MOUNTAINS ROSE TO THE WEST; big blue, magnificent pyramids. A whole city of them. Even now in late August, there were a few high peaks where one could spot the occasional splotch of white where the snow never melted. The Indians called it the Backbone of the World, and Levi thought that was a fitting name.

It had been two weeks since they started North. How many miles Levi could not say, although he would guess they'd averaged twenty or so a day. It was a brisk pace, but not undoable for the little Indian ponies. They were used to traveling, and hardy, and could've done an extra ten if Levi had wanted to push them.

Water was plentiful and for every river they crossed, they found a dozen streams or creeks. Elk, deer, bison, antelope; the whole area teemed with game, and a hunter had naught more to do than pick a direction and shoot should he have a taste in mind. The sun was warm, and the afternoon storms gave plenty of warning. This was indeed a land of plains and meadows.

The Old Man trailed behind him, stony faced and solemn. Truth was, Levi had taken a liking to the old Indian. He reminded him of Ol' Mohe, his Cherokee uncle. Mohe hadn't been blood, but he'd treated him as such, more a father to him than his own at most times. Mohe had taught him how to ride, how to track, how to hunt, and how to fight. What more could a father teach a son?

But Mohe had taught him of curses as well. His tales of the little folk or the moon eyed people, or never camping on mounds and how they were the burial places of giants and long-ago folks even though they just looked like hills now.

But Levi had grown up from mountain folks, already a superstitious bunch. A people prone to belief in witches, haunts, and fae. Some said the mountains were the same from back home, from those in Ireland and Scotland. Once, Levi had asked how they could know such things, and his father had simply said, "the haunts are the same."

There was an old woman who lived on the mountain back home. Folks were scared of her; said she'd made a deal with the devil when her husband died. People would go up the mountain when they got right desperate with all sorts of ailments. They'd usually bring an animal or something, a prized one, the best they had, and take it up with them, but they'd never return with it. Folks said she sacrificed them to the devil. Nobody ever admitted to seeing her right out, but word always got around; usually in whispers. People would lose a prize mule, or a favorite bull would disappear from their farm, but they'd have their child back and in good enough health, ones that had been sickly their whole life.

Then there were the tales of bright lights visiting in the middle of the night; orbs and such. Some said that was fae folk. Others said it was angels and such. Again, who could know. The Smokies were haunted. Of that much Levi was sure.

Mohe used to say that spirits were bound by lands, that one spirit lost its power in other places. Said the same way men divided the earth, the spirits carved up the above and below places. And this seemed to track with what the preacher said on Sunday, with Hebrews conquering the lands of Canaan, and Canaan protected by its own gods.

But again, who could know?

By this time, they were clear of the Ute territory, had skirted right along the edge of the Lakota's range, and were well into Crow hunting grounds.

The Indians had no formal boundaries of course, but that made their territories no less well defined, much the same way a lion marks out his section of the mountains. Yet, the edges were always in contention.

Most of them didn't bother him, or any of the other trappers for the most part. There was no real sense of danger in a lone man or two crossing through. No threat to their hunting grounds. Besides, they liked to trade. The only real danger was looking like a target. Again, lions being an apt comparison. Cougars would most always rather leave a man alone then tangle with him, lest he threaten her cubs or make himself look like easy prey. Of course, man-killers once started, rarely stopped, and the same for murderous men.

And that was the logic to the bloody, feathered scalps that hung off the side of his saddle, which he dangled as advertisement. They said he wasn't an easy mark and served a warning to any young bucks looking for an easy coup. But there was more to it than that. It let them know he was capable of living in their land, by their ways. Tangle with him, and there would be no qualms about matching savagery for savagery. It was in short, a simple type of respect.

Past the Crows were the Blackfoot. There was a Crow summer camp, which they would likely reach tomorrow. There were a pair of trappers that had taken wives of the tribe and lived there now, Ben Murphy and Tanglefoot Riley. He had a mind to stop in and trade stories, maybe do a bit of trading, but mostly see what he could find out about the Blackfoot camps.

They camped that night by a small creek, no doubt fed by a spring further on, and built a small fire down in a draw where it could not be seen, even from the high points of the land. The place was hidden well enough, either side screened by Cottonwoods and a tangle of Juniper.

Levi tended his shoulder, which had begun to smart. It had been healing nicely, or so he thought, but then Jack Wagon had spooked while Levi was trying to load him up. The animal had thrown his head back and whipped his body around while Levi adjusted the animal's the cinch. The movement had jerked the whole damn wound open, and it looked nearly as bad now as it had when he'd first been shot.

He dressed the wound using the jug of shine he kept on the back of the mule. A trick that one of the mountain healer's back home swore on. He didn't know what it did, only that it stung all to hell, and he'd never really had a cut fester. It would be healed already if it didn't keep getting opened up. When he was done cleaning it, he replaced the cork, and put his shirt back on.

"Drink?" the Old Man signed.

"No," Levi signed back. Last thing he needed was the Old Man on crazy water.

The Old Man gave a dour look, and then slumped back against the log he'd positioned behind him.

Levi secured the jug in the pack of supplies and sat down. "Why are you so far South?" he asked.

"I will die soon, and my spirit will go off." The man motioned to the east. "I have things to do before I go."

"What makes you think they won't just kill us?" Levi asked. Levi hadn't known the Blackfoot to be friendly with Lakota. In fact, he hadn't known them to be friendly with just about anyone. What the Comanche were to the South, so the Blackfoot were to the North. They were raiders and hunters first. Farmers only as far as planting a few patches of tobacco in an undisturbed location counted as farming.

"They will not?" The Old Man replied. "You walk with the Coyote."

"What does the Coyote have to do with anything?" Levi signed back.

"It came to me in a Vision. It said go with the one that walks with the Coyote. He will show you peace."

Levi ran a frustrated hand through his tangled hair, then signed furiously, "A vision?"

The Old Man just shrugged.

"Do you have kids?" Levi signed.

The old Indian held up seven of his fingers, his eyes sparkling. And then he put four of them down, and motioned off to the east in the direction spirits go.

Levi simply nodded that he understood.

They remained silent after that. Levi stared into the fire, watching the flames dance and sigh. Fires calmed him. They drew him deep into his own thoughts, but never left him worse off for the exercise. The Old Man rolled over after a while, drawing his buffalo robe up around his shoulder.

DAWN HAD JUST CRACKED THE SKY WHEN Levi rose from his bed of grass and dirt. The Old Man was gone, and in the place he'd lain was the crumpled Buffalo Robe. Levi stirred the coals to the fire and didn't think much of the missing Indian. It wasn't until the coffee was boiling that he became curious about the man's whereabouts.

He did a circle around camp, and then went wider, until he found the old man passed out naked under a tree, the jug of shine laying on its side next to him, the cork nowhere to be found.

"Dammit," Levi said. He snatched the jug up and turned it over, watching a single drop circle the rim before falling.

The Old Man snorted violently, and then settled back into a deep snore.

That was the only shine Levi had. Had cost him a pretty penny too. He needed it for his wounds, but more than that, he could use it to sweeten a deal with one of the tribes should he find himself in trouble.

Levi thought for a moment about leaving the old man right there in the prairie and taking off. But he couldn't, not after the man had returned Jack Wagon to him.

He took the empty jug to the creek and submerged it, watching it belch air and gulp the clear water. Then he wandered back to the old man and tipped the jug over him, until he came sputtering to life. He was madder than a pack of hornets when he woke, then he saw the jug, then he rubbed bloodshot eyes, and shook his head like a great old bull elk who'd been caught on the wrong side of the rut.

"Get up. We're moving." Levi said.

They drank their coffee in silence. The Old Man didn't say nothing about the jug, but once he started to complain about his head, and Levi signed back to him that he wished it would fall off completely.

Old Man shut up after that.

The sun was high in the sky when they made it to the Crow camp. They approached it slowly and in clear view so the tribe knew they weren't there to sneak around or do anything untoward. This was the camp of the Kicked in the Bellies Crow. A strong, warlike people, despite their name, or maybe on account of their name. Levi didn't know.

A pack of young braves ran up to them, and their horses were swarmed by boys no older than ten. Levi greeted the men, and signed that he was there to trade, then he asked about the white men.

One of the boys ran off, and they sat their horses at the edge of camp, while the Crow braves milled around, looking them up and down suspiciously. They looked sternly at the Old Man next to him, and Levi wondered if bringing a Lakota here was going to be a problem.

Then Tanglefoot came walking through the throng, and shouted to them, and waved his hand, a broad smile breaking up the red beard that reached to his chest.

Levi slipped off his horse and grasped the man's outstretched hand. "How you been you old bastard."

"Can't complain," Tanglefoot said. "Been an easy summer. Who's this." He motioned towards the Old Man.

"I don't know his name. Just call him Old Man," Levi said.

Tanglefoot laughed. "You still picking up strays. Like that coyote, you used to run around with."

"Loki still comes around," Levi said. "Probably hanging around out there now. Where's Murphy?"

"He's out hunting the mountains," Tanglefoot said. "Be back in a few days if you have a mind to still be here." Tanglefoot motioned for him to follow, then led them through the throng of Indians that had gathered.

He said something to them in their language and they laughed, some smiled, then slowly dispersed.

They sat outside Tanglefoot's lodge, and his woman brought a pipe and a small pouch of tobacco. She was a proud looking woman, with hair as black as night, and dark, perceptive eyes. She wore an otter skin dress, bleached white, and decorated with little red beads in the shape of flowers and birds. Tanglefoot lit the pipe with a stick pulled from the fire, and then puffed silently before passing it to Levi.

"Where you been?" Tanglefoot questioned.

"Spent the summer down south," Levi said. "Did a might hunting and fishing, traded a few wild mustangs off to the Arapaho. Set up another winter camp in a little box canyon."

"Sounds busy," Tanglefoot said.

"A might," Levi responded. "Headed North now."

"Trapping?"

"Blackfoot lands," Levi said. "They got a healer there."

Tanglefoot shook his head in dismay. "What you want with the Blackfoot?"

Levi told him about the curse, and the Ute graveyard, and how the Old Man had heard tell of the Medicine Woman among the Blackfoot, the one with the power to lift curses. Conspicuously, he left out the part about him being born under a dark star or his passing belief in fae. Most men of his sort snorted at the supernatural.

"I ain't heard nothing about no Medicine Woman up there," Tanglefoot replied. "But I do put stock in curses, and once you pick one up, you best git rid of it soon as possible. These ain't Christian lands, and these people are heathens, even if I do like them. But you don't want nothing to do with the Blackfoot right now."

"Why's that?" Levi asked.

"On account of them pissing in everyone's pot," Tanglefoot said. "They raided here no more'n two weeks ago, stole a pile of ponies and killed the Chief's son. I'd keep that bit about you visiting them between you and me. They're fixing to have a council about it tonight."

"When they headed out?" Levi asked.

"Shit if I know," Tanglefoot said. "You know how these things go. Could be tomorrow or could be next month. They got to test their medicine and talk everything to death. Work up their courage like. But I'd expect it to be sooner than later this time, on account of White Bear's nephew, Charging Bull. He's mighty worked up about it, and the people respect him. He's out to make a name for himself."

"Think we'll best be gone by morning," Levi replied.

"But tonight we smoke and eat," Tanglefoot said. He looked at Levi inquisitively and a little too hopeful. They spent the rest of the night there, smoking, and telling tales. Red Deer made them a dish of buffalo steak and blood pudding which they put down easily.

Someways off, the war council took place around a blazing fire. Braves took turns speaking, and even though Levi couldn't understand a word they said, he got the sense that they were indeed working themselves up.

At different turns, the council raised their voices, occasionally talking over each other, before someone got them to settle back down. All of this punctuated by the occasional bout of singing and dancing, and every so often the fire would blaze brighter, throwing sparks in the air as some young boy fed it more logs.

Levi passed the pipe between him, the Old Man, and Tanglefoot. The council struggled long into the night. Levi fell asleep before the Kicked-In-The-Bellies had quit.

CHAPTER 6

SNAKE MEDICINE

By midday they were on the move, horses loaded down with rolls of buffalo hide and lodge poles. Some dragged travois loaded with household items. The children threw rocks at each other, and rode stick horses alongside their parents. Little boys pretended that they were already on the hunt as they ran alongside.

When they arrived at their new camp site, Large Teeth unloaded the buffalo robes that Black Crow had returned. He'd given the gifts back, saying he had made his decision.

"I have chosen Spotted Locust," Black Crow had said. "He gives many horses. Even two Buffalo Runners."

Large Teeth had known it was likely, probable even, given his family's history. But he'd still been taken aback. And he had watched in disbelief as Black Crow departed.

Now, he threw the robes in a pile. He had no need for so many. Black Crow had dishonored him, and the pile of robes before him were proof of it.

He watched Spotted Locust make his way across

the camp. He had many horses for one so young, most given to him by his father. A Buffalo Runner was a fine gift, but two Buffalo Runners was unheard of, even for a girl such as Apaniaki. What could Black Crow do with so much fine horseflesh, he rarely ran in the hunts anymore. Instead, he preferred to lend out his Runners in exchange for the kills.

All of his horses were normal ponies and of no use on a hunt. For the chase, one needed only the finest horse. One that was fast and strong and could run at top speed for miles. For a horse to be a Buffalo Runner it needed three things—courage, speed, and intelligence. It could not fear the Black Horn like other horses did, for it had to run alongside the stampeding herd. It needed speed and intelligence to bring its rider alongside the herd, and the ability to pull away when the Black Horn charged.

Large Teeth kicked a rock with one of his moccasined feet and sent it bounding towards a grove of Aspen. The action stung, but he paid little attention to the pain. He sat down, crossed his legs, and watched as the others worked. The rejected gifts piled up in front of him.

Apaniaki helped Red Beaver set up his lodge at the center of the encampment, and Large Teeth watched her closely. He watched the way a panther watches the deer. She was beautiful. Straight black hair that fell far past her shoulders and gleamed like a Ravens wing. She was not fat, like the old women, but slender, and well-shaped. Her face was not like the other women either, with their crooked noses or thin lips. No, Apaniaki was of uncommon beauty, with almond eyes that shone like the moon. Eyes the color of water, such as he had only heard tales of. Some had thought her to be the daughter of a Long Knife, but she was not, she was Mandan, and many of their tribe had pale features, blue eyes, and sometimes hair like lightning. The Mandan had been here for a long time, long before the White Eyes had arrived. Her beauty was the kind that men fought over; the kind that would make many other braves jealous.

She bent over to pick up a lodge pole, and Large Teeth stared. He had spent many a night thinking about her. Thinking about taking her for his wife. But now she was to go to Spotted Locust.

Large Teeth would be a great warrior someday, that was his only hope. He had not started yet, for he was still without wealth, but war would change that. He would lead raids in the winter, and steal many fine Buffalo Runners for himself, and take many scalps to decorate his lodge. With war honors came respect. And with respect, power. Someday, Black Crow would regret his decision. Someday, Large Teeth would take what was his, and his lodge would have many wives, many Buffalo Runners, and many scalps.

But all of the wives in the world would be no consolation to losing Apaniaki. For she was powerful, and her medicine was strong. Just a portion of it would give him strength in battle. Some even said that she was learning the medicine of the Wood Eater in secret. Very few women had ever learned the songs of the Beaver Medicine bundle. And all of it would be wasted on Spotted Locust.

His thoughts were interrupted by the whinny of a pony, and he made his way to Gray Wolf's lodge. So distracted with winning Apaniaki, he'd neglected making his own arrangements for the hunt.

"Let me help Uncle?" Large Teeth asked. He worried that the offer would ring hollow, as Gray Wolf's lodge only lacked a covering. The difficult task of setting up the poles already complete.

"You come for a runner?" Gray Wolf asked. "You do not want to help."

Large Teeth gave a strained laugh.

"I come for both. The hunt is in two days. I will pay you back as always, with a portion of the kills."

"They are already promised," Gray Wolf said. "You should have come to me earlier, instead of chasing that girl."

Gray Wolf had never liked Black Crow, and by extension his daughter. It had been Black Crow who had lobbied for mercy when he had wanted death for Shining Feathers. And Large Teeth knew he still thought her death would have been better? Now, she wandered camp making herself a nuisance and begging for scraps. Her cut-nose a constant reminder of Black Crow's mercy and Gray Wolf's dishonor.

"I love her," Large Teeth said. "And I am family. You would turn your back on me?"

Gray Wolf snorted. "Find your own Buffalo Runners. You will not have the use of mine."

Large Teeth clinched his fist, and the action was not lost on Gray Wolf.

"Go boy," Gray Wolf commanded. "Before I lose my patience."

Large Teeth took the words in stride, waiting until his back was turned to grimace. His family was a black mark on the tribe. And if not for his family, Apaniaki would be his.

He did not sleep in his lodge that night, neither did he celebrate or prepare for the hunt by the fire with the rest of the tribe. The band would sing songs and beat drums and smoke pipes long into the night. They would tell stories of prior hunts.

They would reminisce about the Dog Days, the days before they had the horse, and Red Beaver would fill their heads with nonsense about the future. The man spoke in riddles and he had long since lost faith in the Medicine Man's powers.

But more importantly, the union of Apaniaki and Spotted Locust would be tomorrow morning, and the hunt would be the day after. The first it seemed he was destined to lose, but if he could not make the hunt, he would have a hard winter and lose much honor.

He tried to focus on his plight at hand, but instead his thoughts kept returning to Apaniaki and Spotted Locust. The thought of them together—of the night after their union—sickened him.

Restless, he slipped off from camp. The moon was high above him. He hiked on an empty stomach to the highest point he could find. It was the top of a high hill, one side a gentle incline, the other a craggy drop, and below him he could see the whirl of torches, and just make out the faintest of songs.

He turned his back on the camp, and he prayed for a vision. One that would show him the way to a Buffalo Runner. He prayed and shouted long into the night, even as the drums from the valley below him faded.

It was early morning when he stopped, exhausted and covered in sweat. He collapsed against the earth, oblivious to the chill of the night's breeze. Then his animal helper came. It was a serpent. He'd seen it many times in his dreams, but he'd never been able to interact with it. He had often tried, but before he could say anything, it either vanished, or he woke up.

Now it came to him, crawling on its belly and he lay paralyzed with fear.

When it was close enough to strike, it transformed into an old woman. She was scraggle toothed and gray, her face held so close to him that he could count the hairs on her lip.

"Your enemy has a Buffalo Runner," the old woman said.

Large Teeth managed a nod.

"Then ask him. Make peace. Peace must always come before war," she continued. Then she removed from the bag on her back, a large bow, and he recognized it as his bow, carved of Yew, and she broke the bow, tossing it aside. Then from her bag, she drew another bow, this one beautiful and made of horn, its limbs wrapped in the skin of the snake.

"You must take your bow," the Snake Woman said. "And cast it aside. For it is not strong enough to hold my medicine. You must make a bow of horn and wrap its limbs with the skin of the snake. But not any snake. The one that rattles. And you will hang the rattle from a leather thong at the tip of the bow, as a warning to all of your medicine. This bow will not break. And it will fire arrows that do not miss. Arrows that pierce the thickest hides, and the most rigid shields."

Then she showed him the dances he must do to honor the snake, and how to renew the bow's medicine.

"You must never let it rest on the ground. At night, it must always be unstrung, and put high up in a place of honor in the lodge. And in the mornings, you must set it outside to soak the first rays of the sun."

Then the old woman transformed back into a snake. And as she slithered away, a locust appeared in her path, and the snake struck the locust, and consumed it.

CHAPTER 7
DOE EYES

APANIAKI SAT BY THE FIRE, SILENT AND brooding. Outside the celebrations grew louder, the people were happy. Tomorrow their Chief's daughter... she... would be married, and then they would hunt the Black Horn's for the last time before winter. They had much to celebrate.

Black Crow and Fox Kitten Woman laughed together. They took no notice of her silence. After a while, Black Crow asked if she would go with them to celebrate, but she declined.

When they left, she broke down in tears.

She would run away, she decided. She would go to Fox Kitten Woman's people far in the North. They would accept her. It would be a long time before they discovered where she had gone, and by that time Spotted Locust would no doubt take another wife.

The moment had come. The one she had denied her whole life, quieting her heart against, and in the end it had not resulted in any more strength. He would be a fine enough husband. He was wealthy, and strong, and had respect among the tribe. That he was highly desired by the other girls, was no secret, for many had snuck away from his lodge before the morning's light.

And she would be his Sits-Beside-Him-Wife, and she would grow old while punishing the younger wives he took for the love she could not feel. This was her path, and the imminence of it wrung a knot in her belly.

She grabbed a brightly colored parfleche from the back of the lodge, her own movements a stranger to her. Hurriedly, she gathered up a a pair of buckskin pants, new moccasins, a knife, a fire bag, and then scrounged through her father's stores of dried meat, before packing it all away in the leather bag.

Apaniaki slipped outside the edge of her teepee. At the far end of camp, a fire blazed, and the people danced and sang. She stood listening to them for a while, and felt a heavy guilt that it was for her. She glanced in the direction of the timber, and felt as if the darkness itself was watching her.

When she was free of the camp, free of the shouting and singing, she found that a big full moon hung overhead, and it lit her path with silver light. Around her, the trees rose in shadows; dark monoliths that judged her for sneaking away, for forsaking her people. She was a nothing person, for she was running away.

Off in the night, Napi screamed, and she froze, ice flowing through her veins. Other Coyotes answered Napi's call with squealing yelps and cries. Apaniaki gripped the bone-handled knife that Black Crow had given her as a little girl, and tried to find her courage.

She continued towards the lake, her nerve already on a razor's edge, when the coyotes screamed again, calling to each other. She sensed a warning in their howls, and she knew that she could not turn her back on her people. She could not be a coward, for that would be a death worse than marrying Spotted Locust. She could not leave her father, whom she so deeply loved, or leave Fox Kitten Woman alone with the grief of losing her.

She collapsed then. And sat for a long while, she prayed that a way would be made for her. She prayed that she would not have to marry Spotted Locust. She prayed for strength should she be forced to.

When she had left all of her feelings with the lonely moon, a lone Coyote called, but none answered back. It's howl was more plaintive, almost sad. She wondered what it was saying, and she wondered why none answered.

She snuck back to camp then. It was late, and the celebration had ended, but the fire still burned large on the edge of the camp. She snuck into the lodge, careful not to wake the sleeping forms of her father and mother. She wrapped herself in the dull warmth of the buffalo blankets, and she stared at the dim blackness of the lodge.

She wept quietly.

Then she heard movement, the soft rustle of furs, and she felt Fox Kitten Woman lay down next to her. A gentle hand stroked her head and Fox Kitten Woman soothed her as she had so often done when she was a little girl. Then Apaniaki grabbed Fox Kitten Woman's hand and squeezed it tight.

It was the next morning when Apaniaki rose, as she often did to bathe. She woke with a renewed strength, and resigned herself to the day ahead.

Slowly, she worked her way down to the lake, passed the spot where she had left her tears the night before, and found a place along the water's edge hidden on all sides with dense reeds. The water was clear and still. It's surface obsidian. Carefully, she removed her moccasins.

She would bathe, and return, and by this evening she would be Spotted Locust's wife. She had made her pleas, and she would make peace with the answer. But she would not grovel at the foot of the universe any longer.

The sun broke the membrane that separated night from day, and its low orange glow cast the mountains and the trees and the sky in blues and grays and shadow.

She tested the water with a bare toe and found it to be just as cold as she had expected. Slowly she peeled off the rawhide dress exposing herself to all of nature and felt the morning wrap around her. She shivered, and continued into the water, letting it take her breath.

She was already up to her chest in the water, and concentrating on her breathing—one deep breath, and a heavy exhale—when she saw him.

IT WASN'T UNTIL SHE PULLED THE DRESS over her head that he caught the movement of her. She stood at the water's edge, testing it with a delicately extended foot. Soft curves and firm tan skin pulled taught over a delicate frame. Black hair that hung past her shoulders, and big doe eyes that seemed to perceive everything and nothing. Breasts, firm against the morning chill–

–Levi looked away, suddenly conscious of the situation, of her nakedness, of his own.

He stood in the water, completely nude, save for the belt strapped about his waist so that he might retain at least one weapon while bathing. His Hawken and clothes lay carefully concealed beneath a tree at the water's edge, and his brace of pistols he'd left behind with the Old Man keeping watch over the horses.

Her appearance had made him the peeping Tom, and he felt a surge of embarrassment at her imminent discovery.

Then he looked back, as he wasn't truly able to look away. Instinct pulled him back–

–She waded into the water, her skin luminescent in the morning's gentle light.

And he felt an urge to alert her to his presence, but his tongue was all caught up in the back of his throat.

Then she saw him, and gasped, eyes wide, and again, he found a doe to be an apt description. But there was something different about her, something he'd never seen before on an Indian. She had steel gray eyes, the color of a lake at dusk. Blue eyes by all accounts, yet, her features were still Indian, from the strong proud jaw to the delicate aquiline nose. And of course, her straight, raven hair. She was a woman of striking beauty.

She froze, and he realized he was just as frozen, just as immobile. The ability to think, to react, stolen from him.

They both stood there, trapped by the other's presence.

A twig snapped somewhere off the bank of the lake and broke the trance, giving him the use of his limbs once more. She started, but he brought a finger to his lips, and gave her a severe look that once again immobilized her.

There was another coming. Someone, concerned with silence. She had heard it too. He noted the anxious heave of her breast, and the gentle flare of her nostrils.

He kept his finger to his lips as her eyes filled with understanding, and he hoped, a reluctant trust.

She did not scream. She did not move.

He submerged himself, and swam swiftly under water, resurfacing just inside a pocket of reeds at the lake's edge. He blinked the water out of his eyes and pulled the knife from its place at his waist. His ears strained for more sounds.

A horse snorted someways off.

Just the top of his head protruded from the water, enough so that he could see and hear and breathe. The woman still hadn't moved. Her eyes had said she wouldn't, and his ears confirmed as much.

Then the whole of his focus centered on the soft sound of padded feet. A Crow scout emerged from the trees in a low crouch. And as he approached, Levi again submerged himself.

The brave knelt at lake's edge. Apparently come to drink, and he showed no sign that he was aware of their presence.

He cupped water in his hand, and was just about to drink, when he spotted the woman, water up to her waist, arms clasped across her bosom, eyes wide with fear.

But before he could do anything, a firm hand wrapped itself around his wrist and yanked him downward into the water.

As the brave's body was snatched underwater,

Levi's blade flashed high, arcing out of it. The girl screamed. And the blade arced back into the water.

The water where they'd both disappeared plumed red.

Moments later, Levi emerged, dragging the Crow from the water by his collar and leaving a trail of blood on the slick rocky bank behind him.

Then he put the knife to the man's hair, slicing and snapping, the action second nature. And the bloody scalp already dangled loosely from his hand when he remembered the girl. He looked back at her, and felt a pang of guilt for taking the trophy in sight of her.

He gathered his clothes and rifle and fled into the trees.

OLD MAN HAD THE HORSES SADDLED AND was smoking a pipe when Levi came stumbling back, naked and out of breath. He held his clothes and Hawken in one hand and the bloody scalp in the other. His knees were scraped all to hell, and one of his legs was splattered with blood from the scalp.

"Crow?" The old Indian signed, pointing at the bloody hair.

Levi hopped on one foot, as he tried to get the leather leggings back on, but since he was still wet, they clung to him. "Look away, dammit. Damn, savages. So free with nakedness."

The old man looked back blankly. Then he signed, "What happened?"

"There was a girl there. A Blackfoot girl, pretty as the moon. She came to the lake to bathe. I killed the Crow scout."

The old man harumphed.

"What's with the paint?" Levi asked, motioning to his partner's face.

"To make peace," the Old Man signed.

Levi paused, wanting to pursue the Old Man's motives further, but decided he had no time to decipher the riddle. They had to beat the girl back to camp if they were to be met with anything other than hostility.

He grabbed the old man by the shoulder and shoved him aboard his horse, then threw himself into his own saddle with a grunt.

They set off through the trees in the direction of the Blackfoot camp. Levi wasn't exactly sure how this was going to work, and it seemed foolhardy just riding up on them. Especially the Blackfoot, as they had taken a disliking to white men, at least those of the American Fur Company.

But he was carrying beads, and knives for trading, and two jugs of whiskey he'd copped off of Tanglefoot, and he hoped to God that would buy him some favor. Besides, he figured riding straight up to them might set them back a foot. Get their curiosity up long enough for him to impress himself upon them.

Or he could always lie, and say he was with Hudson's Bay Company. Blackfoot still traded with them. Not all things were a question of race, but sometimes a matter of allegiance.

As they rode, his thoughts turned to the Indian girl. She'd stirred something in him, something deep within, and he wondered if he should go back for her. If he should help her get back to camp. She'd been beautiful, of course, but it was something else. There was a softness to her, not a weakness, but rather a flawed strength. Flawed by nature's account. A complete and utter vulnerability.

He'd seen a momma deer once... with a fawn.

He'd watched her graze peacefully, as her baby pranced playfully. He'd been hunting of course, and had a taste for venison, but he couldn't pull the trigger. So, he'd simply watched them play. But he'd not been the only one with a taste for venison. And as he watched, a wolf broke from the tree line opposite of him in a mad dash. Had the fawn by its hind leg, quicker than one could say how you doing. The fawn screamed. A most terrible fucking scream. Then the wolf snapped its neck and all was silent.

He'd killed the wolf.

He hadn't known why at the time. And he'd often considered whether it was right or not. The wolf had its claim, and it was a hard thing, making the case that a wolf was wrong for acting the way it was made. But Levi was the way he was made, and there was something wrong with interrupting beauty. And there was beauty in vulnerability. And that day, he didn't like the way the wolf killed the fawn. So maybe in the end, all things were mostly the same.

SPOTTED LOCUST WOKE TO FIND LARGE Teeth sitting outside his lodge.

"My brother," Large Teeth said. "I have come to congratulate you."

Spotted Locust looked at him confused.

"For winning Apaniaki," Large Teeth said.

Spotted Locust grinned and pulled Large Teeth into a hug of thanks. "I know you wanted her too brother, and I am sorry. She is beautiful."

They held each other at arm's length, and Large Teeth said, "It is true, I did want her, but if she had to belong to one—it would be you." The lie galled Large

Teeth, but he had come for a Buffalo Runner, and he would do what his dream required.

Spotted Locust nodded, taking a step back. "Is that what you came to tell me so early?"

"No brother," Large Teeth said. "I have always been a friend to you and have come to ask for one of your Buffalo Runners in the chase today"

"And what would you give me in return?"

"The best cuts of every cow. And this winter, when I plan to raid, you will be the first that I invite."

"It is done," Spotted Locust replied. "But I have no wish to go winter raiding, I have plenty of horses." He added the last part so that his courage could not be called into question. The truth was, winter raids were cold and grueling affairs, and Spotted Locust planned to spend all winter wrapped in a buffalo robe with Apaniaki. He planned to sire a son by summer.

"Thank you," Large Teeth said. "I will not forget this."

"I will give you Star Runner to ride in the hunt."

Large Teeth dipped his head gratefully, then departed. Spotted Locust watched him leave before returning back inside his lodge. From his bed of furs, Dawn Girl stirred. He kicked her gently with his foot, and she groggily asked him who had visited him so late.

"It was no one," Spotted Locust said. "But the people are waking up."

Dawn Girl panicked then and scrambled to her feet. He watched as she slipped into her buckskin dress with not a small bit of pride, for she was very attractive, and he laughed at her hurrying.

"I told you to wake me before morning," Dawn Girl scolded. Hurriedly she pulled on her moccasins.

"Slip out the back and no one will see you," Spotted Locust replied.

"You hope," Dawn Girl said. With a grunt of displeasure, she pulled the flap up at the back of the lodge, checking first to make sure all was clear.

APANIAKI STOOD SHIVERING IN THE WATER. She clutched her arms about her and stared at the spot where the man had disappeared into the trees. He'd stood silently, naked like her, water up to his chest. He'd reminded her of a bear, with his long beard that parlayed itself into the carpet on his chest. She'd never seen a man with so much hair. The braves plucked their beards. Plucked the hair from their chest too. His skin had been pale, whiter than any she'd ever seen. And he'd been tall; a lean man with a strength to him. And he'd handled the Crow scout with what seemed like only one arm and taken the warrior's hair as if an afterthought.

He'd scared her.

But he was only a man. Of a type that she had never seen, and only heard about. He was a Long Knife.

Then she felt the heat rise from her belly, and a flush and flutter climb to her cheeks, and she hid from the surge of confused feelings.

Yet, she wasn't sure that was fair. She wasn't sure she should fear him, for there was a kindness in his eyes. A gentleness. And her own presence had seemed to startle him, even more than it had her. And he'd made no move against her, even as he dispatched the Crow scout.

She slowly moved out of the water and gathered her clothes, pulling on her buckskin dress, still shaking from the excitement. Tremors ran up and down her body, hands quaking, she struggled to secured the bone knife she wore in a belt around her waist.

At the Crow's body, she bent over and inspected the place where his hair had been stolen. She'd never seen a man scalped before. She'd often seen the hair hanging from her father's lodgepole and had often wondered what it was like to take. This reaction to death surprised her. Where the death of the boy, had shaken her, this one had little effect.

Blood did not bother her, for man was like any other animal, made of flesh and bone, and she had gutted many an animal and skinned more—

—the warrior's body heaved upward, reanimated by a deep, desperate breath, and the bloody Crow's eyes came wide open.

Then he grabbed her by the arm, and threw her to the ground, staggering up to his own feet as he did so. She was on her back then, staring up at the mess above her who frantically tried to wipe the blood pouring into his eyes from the top of his gory head.

Apaniaki freed the skinning knife from its sheath, and when the man next threw himself at her, hands outstretched and aimed at her neck, she drove it deep into his breast, letting the weight of him do most of the work.

She lay there gasping underneath the full weight of the warrior's now lifeless body, and then finally, with some effort, she pushed the dead man off her.

She sat there for a long time, not moving.

WHEN APANIAKI FINALLY MADE IT BACK TO camp she found the people already in a great commotion. They'd captured the Long knife and made much talk about his medicine. Napi had saved him, they said. Napi being the People's name for the Coyote.

She wandered through them, hearing bits and pieces of the story.

"He had spoken to Napi," one muttered in a hushed tone.

"The Parted Hair he had rode with tried to kill Black Crow," another said.

They were crowded around in the center of camp. Large Teeth saw her first, his eyes going wide at the sight of her dress, covered as it was with the blood.

He grabbed her. "What happened? Was this the doing of the Long Knife?"

She shook her head no, still in a daze from the morning's events. She felt off balance, overwhelmed with the energy of the mob, and the tale of the Long Knife that came in bits and pieces.

Black Crow came then, and she led him back to the lake, telling him the story as well as she could. She told of going to bathe, and how she had been startled by the Long Knife. How he had killed the Crow warrior, and then ran off into the trees.

Apaniaki stood over the place where the dead Crow had lain. He was gone now. Black Crow squatted over a smattering of blood on the rocks. He dipped his finger in it, and then brought it close to his face before rubbing the blood between his two fingers and smelling it.

"He was dead?" Black Crow asked.

"Yes." Apaniaki said. "I killed him. The Long Knife thought he was dead and took his hair."

"They must have found him?"

"Who?"

"More Crow," her father said, looking around. He slowly stood up and started working in circles around the spot of blood. "The Long Knife killed him?"

“He saved me,” Apaniaki said.

Black Crow grunted.

“What are you going to do with him?” she asked.

“Red Beaver prays for guidance.” Black Crow paused his circles, and knelt, putting his face close to the earth. “Red Beaver says his medicine is too strong, that we would curse ourselves if we killed the one who Napi himself tried to save.”

Then Black Crow started off towards the trees, bent down, and carefully analyzed a smashed clump of grass.

Apaniaki’s thoughts turned to that of the Long Knife. She was worried for him, and she wanted to thank him. She remembered his proud look, and the panther quickness, and the way he’d slunk away, as if a shadow that didn’t want to be seen.

She flushed, and suddenly embarrassed, gave thanks that Black Crow only paid attention to the grass.

It was the same feeling she had on top of a mountain when Cold Maker brought thunder from the north, and her hair stood on end, and her whole body crawled with energy. She decided then that whatever he was, she wanted no part of it, and the best thing she could do was keep her distance.

“We must go back,” Black Crow said. “It was only scouts, but we must be ready.” Then his face softened, and he brushed the hair out of Apaniaki's face, tucking it gently behind her ear. "I am sorry this happened today. We will delay the marriage until after the hunt. A day of happiness cannot start like this."

She averted her eyes, terrified the sparks in them would give away her pleasure. Then she managed a soft, "Ok." And he squeezed her shoulder once more.

“Do you know which way they went?” Large Teeth

asked. He came from the trees, and sidled up next to them.

Black Crow pointed at the gap in the trees. "South. At least three of them."

"I will go after them," Large Teeth said.

"Take Gray Wolf," Black Crow said. "Perhaps this is retribution for the Bloods raid. Report back to me by evening."

Large Teeth nodded.

CHAPTER 8
THE PRISONER

When Levi woke, the first thing he noticed was that all the light had gone out from the world. He had dreamed that he was dying. Drowning to be exact. Death had been a furious river of dark water and white rapids, and he hadn't been able to breathe.

But breath is what brought him back to the land of the living. A deep breath, and then he was here, on the other side, where darkness was everywhere, and the sun peeked through a tiny hole in the sky... the roof—a roof.

The scent of a recently doused cookfire, and stale furs, and earth, and sweet grass hit him in a wave. A frenetic confirmation of life.

As his eyes adjusted, he slowly recognized the inside of a lodge. Flat blank walls painted with scenes of animals, bedding of buffalo skins on the floor, and in another corner a medicine bundle suspended by rawhide cords.

He tried to move, but his hands were bound to the center pole at his back, which explained the sharp pain in his wrists and the numbness of his hands.

"Old Man," he whispered into the dark.

No one answered. Then memory reasserted itself and he remembered the Old Man being struck down violently. It was all a bit foggy due to the pounding in his head.

They had ridden into the Blackfoot camp, announcing themselves loudly at the edge of it. They had stood their horses and waited. The Blackfoot had obviously seen them coming, for the women and children were hidden somewhere out of sight. Slowly, the braves emerged from both the timber and the lodges, surrounding them, bows drawn, and arrows nocked.

Levi had locked eyes with the nearest, accidentally trapping himself into a contest of wills. The arrow fitted onto his bow held a jagged point cut from a hoop of pig iron. Two fingers wrapped around its sinew string. His arm wound tight as a spring, ready for release. His elbow held next to eyes that were cold and dark, his face weathered and beaten, his jaw set, and his lip upturned in aggression. He was naked to the waist, and his skin was tight, showing every small muscle strung just beneath its surface.

The appearance of an older Blackfoot man broke the stare down. He wore a brilliant war bonnet of eagle feathers, exited from one of the central teepees, and stood before them.

"I am Black Crow, why have you come?" the man called.

Levi was just about sign that they had come for trade, when the Old Man next to him broke into a loud strange chant—his death chant. Levi recognized it as such immediately. And then the Old Man had given a war cry, and heeled his horse forward towards the Chief.

The charging horse had barely made it two strides before a near brave put his shoulder firmly into the side of it, knocking the horse sideways, while reaching under the beast's neck to draw the far rein. The brave cranked hard on the horse's neck, torquing it towards the earth, laying the Old Man's mount down in one swift and easy motion that sent its rider tumbling.

Two more braves descended on the Old Man then, war clubs raised, even as the pony struggled back to its feet, but the Chieftain raised a hand and commanded them no. They dragged Old Man off, beating him lightly as they did so.

Levi's own horse shifted its feet nervously at the commotion, and Levi tried to quiet it. He thought that maybe he should turn and run. Maybe, take his chances elsewhere, but the curse hung heavy in his mind, and when he set out to do a thing he'd made it a habit to see it through.

When the horse finally settled. He sat it silently, stoically, and made no move towards his weapons. Indians respected the brave. But they hated fools. Levi had hoped they would see him as the former.

With the Old Man gathered up, several of the braves started towards him. He slid out of the saddle, palms forward, weaponless, to show that he was still peaceful.

They had a look in their eye though, the kind that sparked with hate, and as they descended upon him, it took every fiber of his being not to pull the pistols from his saddle and start on them.

But then there was a yelp and a howl from his peripheral, and a beige blur shot into the approaching braves with a snarl. One of them went down, toppled by the force of the animal, and then Loki was standing in front of Levi, his hackles raised. The braves scurried backwards, and the coyote gave a low whining growl.

"Get out of here," Levi shouted at the coyote. "Git, Loki."

The coyote gave a backward glance, and Levi again commanded him to flee, terrified that an arrow would end the loyal dog.

And then Loki ran off, disappearing into the trees, nearly as quickly as he had appeared.

The Blackfeet stood around him. They broke into a great fearful murmur. Yet, still they circled, but now more warily, keeping their distance, and what had been looks of hate had turned to that of curiosity and some of fear.

Then he remembered hearing the woosh of the club behind him. He'd heard it crack hard on the back of his skull, but even then the sound was already far off, like it had cracked against someone else's skull and not his own. His vision had tunneled quickly, and then he was drowning in a river, and when he'd finally caught his breath, he was here, in this lodge with its very tiny sky.

With a clearer head he took account of his surroundings. The lodge was sparsely furnished. He sat on a buffalo robe, and in front of him was a small stack of brightly covered parfleches neatly stacked on top of each other. A shield hung to his left, and next to it a bow made of Yew, decorated with cherry bark and feathers. Beside it, hung an otter skin quiver decorated with little copper beads and porcupine quills. He took all of this in, and then tried his bindings again.

As he strained, he felt the wound in his shoulder pull open from the effort, and he let out a smart short grunt of pain. He felt the warm wetness of his own blood as it trailed down his armpit and onto his ribs. It felt like sweat and he wondered how long he'd been out. His head pounded, and throat ached, and he wanted water. He wondered if all this was just one more sign of his curse.

Levi heard shuffling outside, and then the flap of the teepee was thrown open and two braves pulled a bundle in and dropped it on the dirt floor. Then they left. As his eyes readjusted to the gloom, the bundle groaned, and Levi realized it was the Old Man. He'd been hogtied and had a nasty lump growing up out of his old wrinkly head.

Old Man was in a bad way. Levi heard the faint rattle of breath. The lump grew and grew, and he wondered at the fact that the man's paper-thin skin never burst wide open and spilled the lump. He felt bad for him, even though he was hardly soft of heart, but old people, and children, and most women... well it just never felt good seeing them get hurt. When a man gets hurt, it just seems to be what he was made for. Taking damage. It may piss a man off if'n it's his brother or a dear friend that gets hurt, but it never really seems unjust. That was it, Levi thought. It was the unjustness of it all.

The Old Man snorted himself awake, then groaned, struggled against his bindings, and then finally his eyes settled on Levi.

"Welcome back Old Man," Levi said. "What was all that about?"

The old man smirked dourly, and the movement seemed to pull at the lump on his head, causing him to wince. He said something in his own language, but Levi couldn't understand it, and signing was impossible due to his arms tied behind his back.

He wondered though. At the Old Man that lay across from him, and at the fact that he himself was still alive. He couldn't quite piece together how they were still breathing. The Old Man had made a good play at ending any peaceful chances they had, but here they were. Unless of course, they were saving them for something, like a few rounds of torture and then execution. Levi swallowed hard, and thought of the curse.

"You were born under a dark star Levi Thurston."

NIGHT HAD FALLEN, AND TWO BRAVES dragged Levi out of the teepee. He stumbled at the door, and they let him fall. With his hands still bound behind his back, he smacked the dirt hard, cutting his lip, and taking the brunt of the fall on his already bleeding shoulder. They hauled him back up, and dragged him towards the center of the camp.

Several fires blazed, casting the camp in an eerie orange hue. Women and children shouted at him, and one of the children ran up with a stick and walloped him on the head. One of the braves dropped him again in order to shoo away the little child, and again he braced himself for impact, but this time the other held him tight.

His feet were still bound, and he felt every rock that they dragged him over, until they came to a large lodge, and they unceremoniously threw him inside, again letting him fall on his face.

An old man stood up and chased them away. Then he turned Levi over, so that Levi lay flat on his back. The old man took out a knife, its white bone handle glittering in the firelight, and Levi squirmed again against his bindings. The old man shushed him with a knowing smile, and then cut open his buckskin shirt.

Levi glanced around the shelter. It was a medicine lodge. The walls painted with images of beavers, birds, buffalo, and horses. He smelled sweet grass burning and with it caught the scent of aged tobacco. A heavy bundle of beaver fur in one corner. He heard a shuffling from the entrance to the lodge behind him.

She sat down next to him. The girl from the lake, but this time fully clothed, yet no less beautiful. Maybe even more beautiful. Her gray-blue eyes sparked in the fire's light, and she avoided his own eyes even as he searched hers. A flush worked its way up her neck, fighting for ground on her cheeks.

The woman and the old Indian exchanged glances, and then words that Levi couldn't understand, for he only knew a paltry few in the Blackfoot language. She left, and he felt a sudden desperate loneliness. A confusing loneliness. And wished for her back.

The old man poked and prodded at his shoulder, and it radiated heat. The pain climbed down his arm to the tip of his fingers, and up the back of his neck where it combined with the thumping in his head.

After a little while, the girl returned, kneeling beside him, and helped the old man arrange a poultice on his shoulder. He realized then that this was the young medicine woman he had come seeking. He felt her hands on his chest. They were warmer than the old ones. He again searched her eyes, and finally catching them, looked away suddenly, like a dog that had not expected to catch whatever he was chasing. And when he chanced another look, she was blushing, and what he thought was a smile tugged at the corners of her mouth.

He grunted as she pressed on his wound, and felt the sweat break out on his forehead, and he realized then that he was forgetting to breathe, trying as hard as he was to not cry out at the pain. He took deep heavy breaths through his nose but they barely helped.

When he looked back at her and saw a flicker of concern in her eye, and he felt exposed and helpless, more naked than he had at the lake.

Then she left again.

He gave a sideways glance at the small hand axe the old man had used to grind and mash the poultice. It was barely within reach. A quick shifting of his body, or perhaps a distraction, and he could palm the small stone tool.

He eyed the brave that stood guard by the door. The man watched him, hawk-like. Predator's eyes, beady and black, traced his every movement, followed every forlorn expression, and searching every place that his eyes happened to linger. The brave's body was lean and knotted, and he grasped a colorful war lance ready to run him through at the slightest sign of struggle.

Then before he could find his moment, the other braves appeared at the door, descending on him quickly to haul him up and away.

But as they did so, one stumbled, and Levi took the opportunity to overreact, falling roughly back down to his knees, smashing the little clay mixing bowl, and covering the small stone axe with his body.

The other harumphed at his clumsiness, and cuffed Levi in the side of the head with a cupped hand. The old man scolded the brave in a stream of Blackfoot word that Levi could not comprehend. They hauled him away after that, and tied him back up to the center pole of his prison lodge.

He sat in the darkness, the lodgepole at his back, and somewhat hopeful that he would make it out alive. He needed a way to communicate what he'd come for, to tell them about the curse...

...then what? Be gone, he thought, and that answer didn't quite sit right, because it didn't include the girl with the moonlit eyes. Or he could just escape. Leave this place now and never return.

He turned the small stone axe over in his hand. The sharp edges bringing him satisfaction as they scraped his skin.

CHAPTER 9
THE HUNT

A LITTLE BEFORE MIDDAY THEY DEPARTED. The men rode ahead, mounted on their Buffalo Runners, while the women trailed behind.

Large Teeth wore a sleeveless elk-skin shirt decorated with trade beads and porcupine quills. It was his hunting shirt, and was strong medicine, having previously belonged to Gray Wolf. The quills, dyed in reds, yellows, and blues, were arranged in the shape of flowers, and the shirt was to only be worn on Black Horn hunts lest it lose some of its power.

Spotted Locust pulled up alongside Large Teeth and asked, "What do you think Black Crow will do with him?"

"Who?" Large Teeth asked, momentarily confused.

"The Long Knife," Spotted Locust said. "They should kill him, if not for him, Apaniaki would already be my wife."

"Red Beaver fears his medicine," Large Teeth said. "And Black Crow does whatever the old man says."

"Tch!" Spotted Locust huffed. "He is a White Eyes. He has no medicine. We should ask Gray Wolf to call a council and force the issue. The people will listen to him, and he is not afraid to speak his mind."

At this Large Teeth said nothing.

As they neared the herd, the women and children broke off from the group, leading their regular ponies off towards the trees, where they would wait until the killing was done and they could help with the butchering.

When the women and children were out of sight, the hunters lifted the heavy buffalo robes they had draped over the rumps of their horses and used them to cover themselves. Crouching low on their mounts, they were now disguised as Black Horns themselves. Then the hunters, nearly twenty of them, all peeked out at each other from below the Black Horn capes, grinning as they rode forward.

And the Black Horns, a black bubbling mass in front of them, paid no mind to the hunters, believing them to be part of the herd. As they were downwind, the dust and rank smell of a thousand buffalo reached the hunters. Their Runners snorted and pawed in anticipation, their ears perked, and nostrils flared as they prepared to run.

Then time slowed for Large Teeth, and every one of his senses started to work overtime. The click of hooves on stone, the scuffle of their legs as they walked through the tall grass, the powerful bunching and rippling of horseflesh as it moved beneath him, or rather, became part of him. The smell of horse, and meadow, and blue sky. The grasshopper clinging to a blade beneath him, the startled crackle of its wings..

Then Gray Wolf chirped twice, giving the sign to ready, and on his third call the hunters cast off their robes and nocked their arrows.

With whoops and hollers they charged the Black Horns before them. And the near part of the herd, boiling in panic, bawled angrily, finding themselves caught between the hunters and the rest of the milling herd. It was not until the killing and bawling had reached a crescendo that the rest of the herd finally decided to move, and when they did, there was no stopping them, for they took off down the long valley, hooves pounding like an even rolling thunder.

Then Star Runner brought him alongside a fat-looking cow and Large Teeth fired an arrow at the animal. His shot connected just behind the cow's foreleg even as Star Runner pulled away smoothly from the great stumbling beast.

Pulling another arrow, Large Teeth fitted it to his bowstring, with Star Runner keeping pace. Again, Large Teeth shot, and again, his arrow struck home, this time crumpling the cow.

The herd was moving good then, at an all-out run, and someways in front of him, Spotted Locust downed a big black bull.

Large Teeth steered Star Runner back into the herd, clutching him tightly with his legs, and the horse dove forward, galloping headlong at the raging mass of Black Horns. It was then that Large Teeth fell in love with the animal. For he'd ridden none like him, and even after such a short time on his back, he fully trusted the horse's instincts.

He fired his arrows quickly then, one right after another, whooping with each hit and losing track of how many animals he downed. The other hunters did the same, their horses darting in so they could release their arrows, and back out so they could reset. Each time they fired, another Black Horn fell.

Large Teeth had downed five more cows before he realized that he and Spotted Locust had taken the lead, far outpacing the other hunters. He fired off another arrow, this one taking a cow in its shoulder, and as the wounded cow bellowed in pain, a bull broke off from the herd to defend her. As the bull charged, Large Teeth failed to react, finding he could do nothing but brace for the moment the big bull would plow into him.

But Star Runner needed no decision, no thought, nor judgment; but spun away on instinct, so expertly and so abruptly, that he tossed Large Teeth clear of his back. And then Large Teeth, for his part, caught a handful of the horse's red mane, and using the momentum of the fall, bounced his feet off the ground and back onto the horse.

A glance behind him confirmed that the bull had given up. And the old Black Horn, left to shake his giant shaggy head, blew forcefully at the departing horse and rider.

Large Teeth whooped loudly, filled as he was with power and energy, and he shook his bow behind him, back at the frustrated animal.

THE OTHER HUNTERS HAD FALLEN FAR behind him now, and were hidden away by the herd's dust. Large Teeth caught up to Spotted Locust, who continued slinging arrows into the herd.

A cow fell with a great thump and the charging herd split around her.

Spotted Locust, upon seeing his friend, slowed his horse and shook his bow at him, overjoyed and filled with excitement.

Large Teeth's head buzzed, and he shook an excited fist back, before heeling his horse back into a gallop.

They were both racing forward then, neck and neck, the horses no longer competed with the herd next to them, but with each other. Their bodies stretching and retracting in a hard run.

As they ran, Large Teeth remembered his dream. And the image overpowered him—the image of the Snake eating the Locust. And he reacted to this remembrance without thinking, without considering. In fact, he did not react to it at all, but rather something outside of him reacted. Something that took his limbs and puppeted them, so that it was as if he was piloted by an evil spirit.

Long Teeth whipped his horse sideways into the side of Spotted Locust and Night Runner.

Night Runner stumbled towards the charging herd, lost his footing, and tumbled sideways, colliding with a cow.

Star Runner galloped forward, no worse for the collision, and Large Teeth swung the horse away from the edge of the herd, drawing up hard on the reins. So hard, that the horse dropped his rump and dug his hooves into the hard packed prairie, throwing up sod and gravel in order to complete the sudden stop.

Then Large Teeth shifted in his saddle, and straining forward, hands cupped over his eyes, tried to catch sight of the friend he'd just un-horsed.

Night Runner, struggled to rise, one of his legs broken, the Black Horns running past him. Then a great bull charged into the side of the wounded horse and gored the once proud and beautiful animal.

Spotted Locust was still nowhere to be seen. At least not until a flash of tan buckskins caught Large Teeth's eye.

The man was up. And he dodged left and right as Black Horn after Black Horn passed by. Then he dodged again, but a little too late, and he was ragdolled backwards by one of the hulking shadows.

The whole herd shifted closer then, its edge pulsing past the bodies of the man and horse.

Large Teeth dismounted. He squatted on the ground as the herd passed. His breath was all balled up in his chest and his temples throbbed. He felt sick. He knew why he'd done it, but not how. Or what doing it meant for him. Again, the image from his dream accosted him; both comforting him, and hollowing him. The snake striking the locust. The crunch of its brittle body as the snake drew it deeper into its pink mouth. Its neck and body pulsing as it swallowed.

When the herd had passed, and the dust still hung heavy in the air, Large Teeth found the body of Night Runner some fifty paces off. Then he found the broken form of Spotted Locust. And to his surprise, there was still breath in the man's body. Blood foamed at his mouth, and his limbs lay at odd angles, broken in multiple places.

He saw the white bone of a broken and bloody leg.

Frantic now, Large Teeth looked around to make sure none of the other hunters were nearby, and he found none for the dust hung around him thick as smoke.

Then he found a stone, partly buried in the hard packed earth, and he clawed it up, even as his nails filled with grit and dirt. He was frantic, and pawed at the stone the way a hungry animal might try to break into a nest or den. Then he took the stone in his hand, shifting it for a good grip, hefting it, and feeling its weight. He breathed hard, and he bashed the stone into the side of Spotted Locust's head and kept bashing until the breath was no longer in his body.

Quickly, he replaced the rock in its hole, careful to place the bloody side down.

His hands were covered in blood. He wiped them in the dirt, turning the blood to mud. Then he just sat down, out of breath, and dazed. After a time, movement drew his eye. It was the body of a rattlesnake—its body curling around itself in death throes, having been trampled to death by the herd.

Large Teeth rose slowly and walked to the snake. He stood over it watching it writhe and curl at his feet, and he felt a deep sadness for it, and felt something of the future in it. It opened and closed its mouth trying to bite its killer, trying to bite and kill anything.

He drew his knife then and cut off its head, and gathered up the body, still writhing, and wrapped it up in a piece of leather. Then he packed it onto the back of Star Runner.

With it, he would make the snake woman's bow. With it, his medicine would be strong. With it, he would make another case to wed Apaniaki.

BLACK CROW AND GRAY WOLF TURNED THE cow over for Apaniaki and her mother to butcher. Fox Kitten Woman cut quickly and Apaniaki gripped the buffalo's hide and peeled it downward. They would leave nothing on this hunt, as they sometimes did on the summer hunt when the young bulls were harvested.

Gray Wolf and Black Crow departed to identify more of their downed animals, looking for the personalized markings on their arrows.

Apaniaki watched as Fox Kitten Woman worked, slicing open the great cavity of the cow. Apaniaki reached inside, locating first the liver, and then the heart. They were slick and still warm. She set the great beast's organs aside on a section of its hide, saving all of it, even the stomach and the bladder, which they would use to make water buckets.

"Are you happy with your father's choice?" Fox Kitten Woman asked.

"He is certainly better than Large Teeth," Apaniaki said.

Fox Kitten Woman laughed. "I know. I impressed that upon him."

"He wasn't really thinking about giving me to Large Teeth?" Apaniaki asked.

"Your father thinks Spotted Locust is lazy," Fox Kitten Woman replied. "He says it is good that Large Teeth is poor. It makes him ambitious, and that he will be a great hunter and feared warrior someday."

Apaniaki huffed.

"Your father loves you. He only wants what's best."

"But I love none of them," Apaniaki said. "I want none of them." Her mind was invaded by the image of the Long Knife standing naked in the lake. She shook her head involuntarily, as if trying to release the image itself. Then she tucked a strand of wayward hair behind her ear.

"But you need them," Fox Kitten Woman continued. "I did not love Black Crow at first. His heart was still with Singing Woman when I was given to him. But he took care of me, and we were hardened together, and now I can imagine belonging to no..."

Fox Kitten Woman had stopped talking and Apaniaki followed her gaze. A rider came towards them, carrying the body of another. The talking and singing of the others stopped as they, too, saw the rider. As they neared, Apaniaki recognized the rider to be that of Large Teeth. In his arms he held the body of Spotted Locust.

CHAPTER 10
PARLAY

IT WAS DARK OUT WHEN HE WENT TO WORK on the bindings. It was slow going at first, as the hand axe was not sharp enough to make quick work of the rawhide. And his hands, being bound together behind him, could not apply much pressure, or even make use the full length of the jagged stone blade. Several times he dropped the stone instrument due to the awkward position of his work. And each time, getting the blade back in hand became a frustrating mix of grasping around for the tool and flopping his body around like a fish.

It had been three days since the Medicine Man and his pretty young ward had doctored him. And for three days, he'd heard and seen little of his captors. Some of the tenderness had left his shoulder, and overall he felt a bit stronger and more capable.

Twice each day, a squaw had brought them food. And twice each day, she had failed to bring enough water. So by the afternoon of the third, his mouth was bone dry and his head throbbed from dehydration. He'd spent hours focusing both on the passage of time and the chance to gulp from the waterskin.

Outside the lodge, a pair of young bucks exchanged guard duty. One sitting during the day, and the other at night. Levi quite liked the night watchman. For often, Levi had woken to the man's carefree snoring.

He continued his work on the bindings, and after a few hours, much sweat, and the occasional grunt of frustration his hands were free. Seconds later, so were his feet.

The old man stared at him, but Levi put a finger to his lips. Then Levi stood, stretched, and looking like a great cat unwinding after a long sleep, shook off his cramps.

When he was good and limber, he crept towards the lodge's leather flap, moving gently in the fall breeze.

Peeking through it, he could see the other lodges, all neatly lined up in rows. Their silver skins reflected the pale moon light.

He steadied his breathing, and listened for the guard. To his satisfaction, the man had once again fell asleep just outside the lodge's door.

Slowly, he stepped outside.

The sleeping guard, slumped against a stump he'd been using as a stool, had his fingers wrapped tightly around a lance. A few feet off, his bow leaned against the lodge's leather skin.

Levi clasped hand over mouth, and snaked an arm around the boy's throat. The young man came awake fighting, but his scream for help came out as a slight wheeze, stifled as it was by the arm around his neck. Levi man-handled the boy then, drawing him into his arms the way a great snake wraps itself around some small prey. He rolled over to his back and sank the back-choke in deeper. And as quickly as the boy had woken, he was asleep again.

Levi shoved the boy off, then lay still for a moment, listening to his surroundings for any sign the struggle had been heard. Nothing in the camp moved.

APANIAKI WOKE TO SOUNDS OF THE FIRE being scraped back to life. She felt the surge of warmth as it chased out the night's chill. Then she snuggled deeper into her buffalo hide blanket as she tried to return to her dreams.

Fox Kitten Woman gave a small gasp, and her Father a fearful grunt, and Apaniaki was wide awake, pushing herself up to see what had happened.

A man sat just the other side of the fire, dropping another piece of wood on its hungry yellow flames.

It was the prisoner. The white man from the lake, here, in their lodge. And then she saw the hostage. Lying next to him, his head almost in the Long Knife's lap, it was Throws Far, one of the young braves tasked with guarding the prisoner's lodge. The man held a knife to the boy's throat, and the boy's eyes were white with fear.

Then the man lifted a single finger to his lips, signaling silence from Black Crow and his family.

Then the man slowly removed his knife from the boy's throat and tossed it to his other hand, where he made a show of setting it down next to him. The brave tried to get up, but could not, for he had been hog-tied hand to foot, and was now left to writhe about on his belly next to the Long Knife.

The Long Knife, for his part, lifted both hands up then, palms out to show that he was no longer an immediate threat and signed, "I have come to trade."

TO LEVI'S SURPRISE, BLACK CROW responded in clear English, "Then talk, Long Knife."

"You know my tongue?" Levi asked, barely able to believe it.

"I know it," the Chief said. "When I was young, I scouted for traders from the North. The Hudson Bay. Now tell me. Why have you come to us. Why have you invaded my lodge in the middle of the night." There was an edge to his voice that made Levi second guess his chosen course of action.

"I seek help," Levi said.

"Have you not found it," the Chief said, pointing to Levi's shoulder.

"Yes." Levi dipped his head in appreciation. "But I have a curse. I took shelter in a Ute graveyard. The dead follow me, or at least that's what the Old Man out there tells me... I fear the evil spirits you people talk about." He caught himself starting to ramble. "I came to find her." He pointed at the Chief's daughter. "I am told that she can remove curses."

The Chief paused at this, saying nothing, then shrugged the Buffalo blanket off his shoulders and shifted his position up towards the fire. He crossed his legs, and sat, as if ready to parlay. His shoulders held straight, and his position upright, as if he'd found some new confidence. "And why should I not have you killed?"

Levi looked from him to the young Medicine Woman, his mind trying to find some reason. "Why haven't you?"

"Because, you rode here with Napi," the Chief said.

"Who's Napi?" Levi asked.

The chief made the sign for the coyote, and then

said, "He is sacred to the People. Some think him the creator. Others, a trickster. Some, think him both."

It was only then that Levi realized how the coyote had saved him. They'd taken one glance at the animal when he came rushing in to help and figured he was big medicine. They hadn't molested Levi for fear of the Coyote.

"The old one you ride with," the Chief continued. "He tried to kill me."

"I didn't know he was going to do that," Levi replied. "He said he had friends here that he wanted to visit before he died."

The Chief paused at this, and then let out a small laugh at Old Man's apparent deception. "You are foolish, like the coyote."

"There's something you should know," Levi said. He was trying to build good will, using anything he had to convince them of his intentions. "The Crow are coming. They are big mad. They sent that scout I killed, and there's more to follow. Of that, I'm sure."

"I sent my braves to track him, they rode several miles, checked many places, there is no war party coming."

"I was there," Levi said. "At the camp of the Kicked in the Bellies when they prepared for war."

"Why should I trust one so friendly with my enemies?"

"I speak the truth," Levi said. "They will come."

"The Kicked in the Bellies are cowards," Black Crow said. "They will do nothing. They bellow and dance, but where are they?" The Chief held out his hands and looked around in mockery.

Black Crow impressed Levi. The way he talked, the way he controlled the situation. There was a wit to him that Levi appreciated. In another life, the two might have rode the river together. Maybe, still—

The Chief snapped his fingers. "Apaniaki, get Steals Many Horses, and tell him to bring braves. Tell him to take this prisoner–"

Levi snapped the knife up, and put it back to the guard's throat.

The girl wavered, caught between her father's orders, and Levi's threat.

"I'll do it," Levi said.

"Then he will die for his Chief," Black Crow said. "And it will be a good death for him. But it will not be a good death for you."

At that, the girl turned and disappeared beneath the back edge of the lodge.

Levi let out a long sigh and set the knife back down next to him. "Lift my curse and I'll leave," Levi said.

"Still, you make demands," Black Crow said, an amused smile breaking across his lips. "You are brave or stupid." The Chief smacked the side of his head using the universal sign for a fool. "I do not know which."

"The Kicked in the Bellies are coming," Levi said. "I know they are."

"Maybe," Black Crow replied. "Or maybe not, either way they will die."

There was movement at the lodge door behind him, and then three braves came barreling inside. They set upon him quickly. Levi did not resist, eating a punch to his kidney that bent him over even as they dragged him up to his feet.

Black Crow said something to them that Levi could not understand, and the flurry of abuse stopped.

CHAPTER 11
FRIENDS TO THE END

APANIAKI LOOKED UP AT THE BODY IN THE tree. It was a lonely tree, someways off from the camp, and away from any others. It was wrapped in a gray and red striped blanket, and a stiff blue hand poked out of the bundle.

The Blackfoot left their dead in tree's so that their soul would not become trapped. They would be leaving tomorrow morning, that way Spotted Locust's soul could find its way to the ancestors in the East and live with them in the Sand Hills.

She gave a tortured look at Large Teeth as he approached.

“I’m sorry,” he started.

Apaniaki said nothing. The lump in her throat had swollen, and her eyes rimmed with tears. She had not particularly liked Spotted Locust, but she had not wished for his death either.

"If I had been there, I would have killed him. Black Crow should have killed him," Large Teeth continued.

Apaniaki realized then that he wasn't talking

about Spotted Locust's death, but rather the Long Knife's attempted escape.

"He didn't do anything," Apaniaki said without thinking. "He didn't even threaten us."

"You defend him," Large Teeth scoffed, suddenly taken aback.

"He thinks himself cursed," she continued. "He asked my father if I would lose his evil spirits."

"But he took the guard," Large Teeth said. "And entered your father's lodge uninvited."

"He is wild and desperate. He does not know our ways," Apaniaki said.

"Then he should be taught," Large Teeth said.

She said nothing, already tired of the conversation.

"Spotted Locust was my friend. My brother. He would have been good to you," Large Teeth continued, changing the subject.

Apaniaki stole a glance at him. He was a liar. They both knew that he loathed Spotted Locust. And they both knew that he wanted to marry her, that he followed her around camp like a lost puppy, always trying to catch her eye. But there was something different about him now, she could sense it. There was an edge, but also a desperation, like something had broken loose inside of him and he couldn't help but chase it.

He caught her look, and their eyes met.

"I am going to ask your father for you."

"Again?" she gasped the words out, catching herself.

"Spotted Locust is gone. You will still need to be married."

They walked the rest of the way back in silence, and every time their hands accidentally brushed each other, Apaniaki drew away in disgust.

She left his side as soon as they reached camp, not bothering to say goodbye.

⸙

SPOTTED LOCUST'S MOTHER SAT BY THE FIRE, her hair chopped short to show the depth of her grief. Gone were the long silver braids that she had long worn. Her face was painted with ash.

Apaniaki looked on in silence. Red Beaver sitting next to her. She was happy that it was dark, and that the firelight did not reach her, for she did not appreciate the curious stares and whispers that came with losing one's soon to be.

She felt sadness for Spotted Locust, of course, but not the sadness for one who was loved, but the sadness that came for an acquaintance, not even a friend.

For the first time since her father had promised her to him, she could breathe. She could breathe full, deep breaths, as the terrible weight of their future together was heaved from her shoulders. And this simple fact made her feel all the worse about it. It was callous she knew, and she tried to deny it. But it was the truth.

After some songs, and as the night wore on, Large Teeth rose and stood in front of the roaring fire. He told the story of Spotted Locust's last hunt. He spoke of how brave Spotted Locust was, and how he had tried to save him. How he had risked his own life by running into the charging herd without fear for his own safety.

"But I was too late," Large Teeth said finally, his eyes moist. "I hid behind the fallen body of Night Runner as the Buffalo ran all around me, and I cried out in pain for I could not find the body of Spotted Locust."

The people listened silently to his tale, some nodded along, and others cried louder for the loss of Spotted Locust. They were moved by the story of their friendship, and for the loss of Large Teeth's friend. Then, Large Teeth told them of his dream, how the snake had given him her medicine, and how he had found the rattlesnake on the day of the hunt. He held it high over his head, and told them of the dream, and how the dream had predicted Spotted Locust's death.

"If only I had the snake's bow at the hunt, I would have saved him," Large Teeth said.

When He-who-kills-many, Spotted Locust's father, having heard all that Large Teeth had to say, stepped forward and thanked him for trying to save his son. He made gifts of Star Runner and Night Runner, Spotted Locust's favorite horses and fast buffalo runners.

Apaniaki pulled the blanket around her tighter, but she found little warmth, for her blood had gone cold. Her father would choose Large Teeth next. He would not hear her reasons.

CHAPTER 12
CROW

THE HIGH-DESERT WHICH HE WAS DREAMING of transformed to hell, and before he knew it, he was coughing and sputtering smoke, and his nose was burning.

He blinked his eyes open against the sting of very real smoke, and found the hide wall of the lodge in front of him on fire. Then he heard them, the loud cry and war whoops of the demons from his dream, the thunder of raider hooves, and the screams of startled women.

He was fully awake then, and pulling against his bindings, but they only cut deeper into his wrists, the rawhide cords having soaked up his sweat and dried tighter.

The Old Man had woken too, and now he chanted, his death chant, wailing at the wall of fire before them.

"Shut up," Levi shouted. For he was sick of the Old Man's death chant, and found it a strange and ignoble tradition, akin to giving up. For in Levi's mind there was always opportunity, and fate would not answer to those not fighting.

Then he heard a shuffle, and felt a nudge, and a figure crouched next to him. It was the girl, the Medicine Woman. He was surprised by her sudden appearance, and confused. Her face was full of fear, and then she took to his bindings with a long knife that gleamed in her hand.

She sawed through the rawhide, taking far too long, and then handed him the knife for the cords around his ankles.

The side of the teepee split open then, consumed by fire, and releasing with it all the smoke that had gathered inside. The parfleches stacked against the wall burst into flame from the sudden exposure to clear night air, and the girl screamed, bolted for the exit and disappeared.

Levi cut the Old Man free, then gathered him up to his feet.

"Shut up," Levi yelled at him again. "We ain't dying yet, don't you see." Then he shoved the old one out into the night.

Free of the burning teepee, it collapsed in on itself, throwing sparks high into the air.

Around them, Blackfoot braves fought on foot against the mounted raiders. Women and children fled, screaming. Some were clubbed down by painted warriors, while still others were scooped up and thrown across their horses. The Crow had come.

A WAR WHOOP WENT UP BEHIND LEVI, AND he staggered around in time to see a painted brave on a gray horse. The horse had a red circle around his eye, and for some reason this was all Levi could focus on as it came bearing down on him.

The warrior swung a stone tomahawk and Levi dove to the ground.

The horse carried its rider past.

Levi picked himself up, caught the old man by the shoulders, and shoved him forward past the dead body of a Blackfoot brave, his body bristling with arrows.

They staggered between burning lodges hunting for the edge of camp and the safety of the woods. Then a scream drew his attention. It was the girl.

She was running for her life, a mounted Crow giving chase. Levi watched, too far away to do anything but pray.

The Crow bent to the side of his charging horse and deftly scooped her up off the ground with one arm before galloping off into the darkness beyond.

She was gone.

Levi was nearly knocked over by a bolting horse then. It was riderless, and reared, kicking its front hooves out violently. Levi grasped the rawhide reins and swung onto its back, thinking only that he would give chase after the girl. The horse spun furiously beneath him, scared and spooked and unsure whether to bolt or buck.

Levi had just reached out a hand to the Old Man when a Crow warrior charged from the opposite direction, leapt from his mount, and tackled Levi to the ground.

They hit the hard packed earth and Levi felt his newly mended shoulder break wide open. He struggled to his knees, left arm dangling uselessly. He dipped his right shoulder in time to block an oncoming kick from the Crow brave's leathered foot.

The warrior stumbled backwards, trying to regain lost balance.

Levi charged him, lowering his shoulder and ducking a late and wild swing. He smashed into the

Crow, shoulder to solar plexus, and knocked him backwards.

The Crow landed flat on his back, and Levi both heard and felt the wind leave the man's body.

He scrambled for the Crow's tomahawk, which had been knocked free in the scuffle, and grasping it, staggered over to the breathless warrior. The Crow lay flat on his back, like an overturned turtle, grasping at his belly, his face pale and contorted like a banked fish as he struggled to reinflate his lungs.

Levi slung the tomahawk once, heard the splinter of skull and bone, winced, and turned away from the violent death throes. He thought briefly about taking the scalp, but then decided that there was no time, and even less reason.

Old Man rode up, having already gathered up the horse, and helped Levi struggle on to its back, his left arm dangling uselessly.

THEY FOUND A THICK STAND OF CEDAR overgrown with long grass, and inside it several deer beds. It was a well-hidden place, on the highpoint of a ridge and allowing escape in several directions, but still thickly covered even as the rest of the forest had started to shed its leaves.

Levi lay flat on his back and stared at an ice blue sky streaked by thin whisps of clouds. He was cold. A chill had descended on the mountains, brought from the North, and he wondered how soon before the first snow. All he wore was what was left of his thin buckskin shirt, cut open by the medicine man and his ward to expose his shoulder. He shivered a bit and got up to pace the heat back into his legs.

Feeling had slowly started to return to his arm, which was good, but the damned thing would never heal if it kept getting opened up. The Old Man sat cross-legged in front of him and stared off into the trees.

They had a scraggle topped and malnourished horse, its rib bones showing, so skinny that if they were forced to eat it, he wasn't sure they'd even get one good meal off it. No blankets. No Buffalo robes. No supplies. No food. Nothing for trade. No guns. A dull knife and a tomahawk with a stone head.

They were used up, Levi thought. And he was still cursed. And the one person who'd been supposed to help him, had been spirited off to God knows where by Crow raiders What was worse—he barely even cared at all on account of the curse and needing her to lift it. No, he cared because he thought she was pretty, and now, with her gone, he felt just a bit love-struck and dumb, and finally able to admit the real reason he'd hung around instead of escaping the other night.

Because at some point, it'd stopped being all about the curse and it started being about whatever that pretty little Indian girl had stirred up in him. They hadn't said more than three words to each other, but for some reason he liked her. And he wanted her bad, in a way that he hadn't fully been able to rationalize. But now she was gone.

A dark star indeed. Hell, a dark sky. Why not a dark and cursed cosmos. That's what he'd been born under.

"Bad medicine—"

"—shut the hell up," Levi said.

He picked up a pebble and hurled it at the Old Man. "This is your fault."

"I go," the Old Man said.

"Fine, but don't you dare touch that horse."

"I don't need the horse. Need to kill Black Crow."

"Good luck then."

The Old Man struggled up to his feet, wandered off through the trees, and was gone.

The wind kicked up. A lonely wind that rattled the dead leaves and howled down through the pass below. The cold, the big icy sky that stretched for miles, the quiet wind, with its loud and all consuming silence. Such were the things that tortured a lonely man.

Levi picked up another stone and hurled it at the trees.

HE SPENT A NIGHT AND A DAY, AND ANOTHER night up on that ridge. Hidden away from the world and licking his wounds. He used the knife to dig out a little hole in the earth where he made a hat full of fire. It had taken him the better part of two hours to build it, using a fire drill and a bow he fashioned using rope he braided out of pieces cut from the pony's tail. Ol 'Mohe had showed him the process when he was no bigger'n thirteen. It was a miserable way to build a fire, but as sure as anything when one had nothing.

He built the fire directly underneath one of the cedars so it's still green branches would break up the smoke. There was a creek that ran through the pass below him, which kept him from thirst. He slept and thought, tended his shoulder, and groaned to himself about his awfully bad luck, and after the first day, hunger got the better of him, so he pulled himself together, and set some snares.

The next morning, he found that he'd caught a hare, so he skinned it out and spit roasted it. It was a better meal than most any from recent memory, which only proved to him that misfortune was one of life's most potent seasonings. With a full belly, and a bit of rest, the mountain was still lonely, but the sun seemed a bit warmer, the sky a bit less ice blue.

He had already decided, really, that he would go after her. The doddling on the ridge had merely been a ploy to convince himself that the decision was his. The Kicked in the Bellies Crow were likely more'n a hundred or two hundred miles south by now, back in the Wind River range they called home. A raiding party could travel fast, covering hundreds of miles in a few days, especially if they'd taken many horses, which the Crow had. They simply switched mounts as they went, having constant access to a fresh one. And after a raid, they rarely stopped until they had returned home, spurning food and sleep for miles.

He wondered if the Blackfoot would go after her. He assumed they would, her being the Chief's daughter, which meant that he would need to get to her first.

Or he could throw in with them? He sat by the fire, watching the flames lap at the fresh sticks as he considered that option.

Without the Old Man around, maybe they would welcome the help. But he knew even as he thought it, that bridge had been burned. The Old Man had seen to that. They didn't trust him, and no amount of explaining would change that.

He glanced at the pony he'd stolen. The bag of bones wouldn't make it more'n fifteen miles a day.

His thoughts turned to the girl. He feared for her. For how the Crow might treat her. She was pretty at least, and smart, and a healer. That played in her favor. If she was lucky, she might even escape being a slave and just be straight up married into the tribe.

Or maybe that was the worse option? He wasn't sure. There were worse fates than being a war bride, but the thought of it made him sick.

He doubted they knew who she was, for if they did, that would mean big trouble. They could kill her as revenge, or try to trade her back, and extract some sort of reparations or maybe even a peace.

As the sun fell, he piled dirt on the fire, making sure it was out. Then he climbed atop the scraggle horse and guided him down the pass. It was time to get moving.

CHAPTER 13
THE RESCUERS

LARGE TEETH PULLED HIS ANIMAL TO A HALT at a small stream where the horse tracks from the Crow party disappeared. He didn't see any tracks on the other side.

"Search up there," Large Teeth ordered. "And Gray Wolf, work downstream."

On the third day after the raid, Black Crow finally gave his permission to take ten braves and the best horses after her. Large Teeth still didn't agree with the delay but he saw the reason in it. Black Crow had insisted that they wait, saying that if they pressed them, they may kill her.

"She must be in their camp when you take her," Black Crow had said. "This is the only way."

Large Teeth watched as the two braves worked their horses up and down the little creek. The others waited behind him, so as not to add their tracks to the trail and confuse it all together. They were a party of ten, all told. And at last, the scouts returned, reporting that they could not find the place.

"It is as if they vanished into thin air," He-Who-Shouts-Loudly said.

"We go straight away then," Large Teeth ordered. It was just as well they'd lost the trail. They knew where the Kicked in the Bellies ranged. They would find them.

He nudged Star Runner forward, and the horse snorted at the water before gracelessly splashing across the stream.

A little further on, past the creek, the horse shook itself like a wet dog, and Large Teeth gripped it with his legs as he struggled to stay its back.

Black Crow had made him leader of the war party. His snake medicine was strong, and the incident with Spotted Locust had won him favor with many in the tribe. He also suspected Black Crow was giving him a chance to prove himself worthy. Worthy of marrying Apaniaki.

Black Crow had given him the brace of pistols taken off the Long Knife and gifted him the rifle as well. Large Teeth wore the pistols draped across his chest, and carried the rifle in his hands. He studied the rifle, thinking of the many enemies that would now fall before him.

They moved on through the country after that, no longer tracking the Kicked in the Bellies but traveling straight ahead towards the mountains where they lived. Summer was over.

The prairie grasses stretched as far as the eye could see, yellowed, and dead, gone to seed. It was wilted by the first freeze, and the whole earth seemed to tremble before the coming of Cold Maker, that Spirit from the North, who brought with him the snows, and the cold, and the hunger. And in the distance, the blue mountains stood somberly, immoveable, indestructible.

At mid-day, they stopped, and made a meal of pemmican, then sat around and smoked their pipes.

Large Teeth, having swapped out his summer buckskins for a thick buffalo robe and hair lined moccasins, looked more like a pile of furs than a man. On his head, which topped the pile, he wore nothing, his ears turning a bright red and burning at Cold Maker's touch. He preferred to have his hearing unimpeded, but Gray Wolf and some of the others wore fur lined caps with flaps to protect their ears.

Gray Wolf sat down beside him. He wore a coat made of wolf's fur, its inside lined with the coarse wool blanket of the Hudson Bay company. When the first snow came, he would switch the coat around and wear it inside out to let the white blanket blend in with winter's landscape.

"This is your first raid," Gray Wolf said. "And you lead."

"Are you mad?" Large Teeth asked.

"You are young, it is true," Gray Wolf said. "But you are kin."

Large Teeth gave a slight grunt of affection.

"But if you fall, I will take command," Gray Wolf added, with a large wry smile. "Have no concern for me."

"You should have loaned me your Buffalo Runners," Large Teeth said.

"I lend to those who don't offend me," Gray Wolf said.

"And now you go to rescue his daughter?" Large Teeth asked.

"Right now she is the whole tribe's daughter," Gray Wolf said. "It is different. In the tribe, we all have a role. Some are enemies one time, and friends another. Some fools are wise men and wise men, fools. You live in relation to others. Do not let others choose your part for you. There is a time and place for revenge, but what good is it, if it destroys everything else you love."

"She will be my wife," Large Teeth said. "I will remember who helped me, and who stood against me."

"Tchk." Gray Wolf clicked, and waved him off.

THEY CAMPED FOR THE NIGHT, HIDDEN FROM the wind in a small gulch rimmed with willows. They camped cold, building no fire for fear it might be seen, and sat close by one another.

Large Teeth guessed that they had covered thirty miles. He was sore, but no worse for wear, for he'd spent all his life on horseback. He sat huddled in his furs and watched the night pass under a cloudless sky. The moon didn't rise until well into the night, and when it did, it cast long shadows on the rolling hills. Somewhere off in the night Napi called, but none of his family called back.

"It is a strange thing, when Napi has no one to call too," Red Horse said.

"It is the Long Knife," Black Horn said. "He and Napi follows us."

"Bah," said Gray Wolf. "Again, with Napi. He would never give a Long Knife his medicine."

"But we saw it," Black Horn said. "Napi protected him."

"Quiet," Large Teeth said. "Gray Wolf is right and I am sick of this talk anyways."

"Tomorrow night, we should be at the foot of the mountains," Gray Wolf said. "We will build the war lodge and you all can tell as many ghost stories you want."

And the next day, they moved on, and when the

flat lands transitioned to long rolling hills, and the mountains loomed overly large above them, seeming so close, yet still far away, they found a place for their war lodge. And as they were near the Crow's winter range, the lodge would be a simple fort where they could stash provision bags for the return to their lands.

The place was heavily timbered and lay next to a small creek fed by a spring from the hill country above them. They had seen Deer and Elk the day before, which was a good sign, for hunting would be quick and easy.

They again spent the night camped in the open, having arrived too late in the day to build the lodge. But the following morning, they woke early, and began dragging dead timbers together and setting them up to form a conical framework. Around the base they laid heavy logs and piled mounds of earth. On top they laid pine boughs and branches, weaving a sturdy roof until the lodge was large enough to sleep all of them.

As the others worked, Lazy One disappeared. He would not help, which is why he had first been called Lazy One; and he no longer worked, because he had been named Lazy One. In such a way, a name begat itself.

But when they were done with the lodge, Lazy One reappeared, saying he had been hunting and that he'd not found anything. It did not go unnoticed by Large Teeth, or the others, that Lazy One had sticks and leaves in his hair, and his manner gave the general impression that he'd been sleeping.

That night they built a fire in the center of the lodge. It smoked at first, stinging Large Teeth's nose and eyes, but he liked the smell, and was hungry for the fire's warmth. It was the first fire they'd felt in four days, and their spirits became mighty once more.

"Tomorrow, Gray Wolf and Steals Many Horses will go and scout ahead to find the Kicked in the Bellies," Large Teeth said.

"And if we don't find them? When should we return?" Steals Many Horses asked.

"Three days," Large Teeth said. "On the third, should you not return, we will come looking for you."

"This is good," Gray Wolf said.

Conversation turned then to prior raids, hunts that had been abject failures, and hunts that had been wildly successful. The night was filled with laughter. Until at last, Large Teeth decided that they would need sleep for tomorrow.

Lazy One tried to lay close to the fire.

"No, you sleep there," Steals Many Horses said, pointing to the very back of the lodge.

Lazy One shrugged, and then dutifully made his bed against the back wall while Gray Wolf snickered.

In the middle of the night, it began to rain and Lazy One woke angry and shouting because the roof above him had not been properly thatched. Lifting his hand, he attempted to reach up and fix it, but instead, that entire portion of the roof fell in, soaking Lazy One as it did so.

Large Teeth, piled more wood on the fire, in order to see what the commotion was all about. The others just woke up laughing.

Lazy One was soaked, dripping water from his hair, and when he saw the others laughing at the hole in the roof, he gathered up his Buffalo coat and stomped out of the war lodge and into the night.

"Will he go?" Large Teeth asked. The others suppressed snorts and chuckles and listened intently to what Laze One did outside.

"Maybe?" Gray Wolf said. "Or just fix the roof."

Then the horses snorted, and then one whinnied, and a few moments later, came the dull clop of hooves. They all laughed even harder.

As it was already early morning, Steals Many Horses and Gray Wolf set off to scout rather than go back to sleep. Large Teeth bid them goodbye and reminded them to return in three days no matter what they had found.

Then, taking his bow, he left camp and worked his way up the sloping foothills in search of game. The black of night gave way to the gentle gray light of morn.

He walked for most of the morning, and by midday, he'd found a place several miles from camp, where Elk grazed peacefully on a far hill. There were four of them, a young bull elk and three cows. The time of mating had already passed, for Cold Maker would come soon, and it appeared that this small herd was newly minted.

Then he worked a wide circle just below the nearest ridge, putting the wind in his face, and the sun at his back, and he ended his stalk no more than forty yards out.

He tucked himself up inside a small stand of pine, where the earth was soft beneath his feet and the smell of pine heavy in the air. Slowly, he nocked an arrow. Felt the fletching as it brushed his hand. Felt the smoothed shaft between his fingers. Every one of his movements becoming small, calculated, and exact. His breathing slowed, his vision narrowed. He ignored the heavy beat in his chest.

The young bull's head shot upward, his nostrils flared and hocks twitched. Then his ears flicked back and forth in search of wayward sound. The cows, for their part, remained largely unaware of danger, and instead focused on their leader, disturbed by his sudden high alert.

Large Teeth froze. Every fiber of his being strung so tight that it felt like he might snap in half.

And at last, the bull dropped his head.

Large Teeth drew and fired the arrow in one smooth motion and the snap-twang of the bowstring set all of them to a run.

He'd felt as much as heard the thwap of it, his arrow, as it connected with the bull's side. And though the bull had run off, he was positive he'd scored a hit.

Moving to the place where the Bull had stood, he looked for blood, and soon found it. It was pink and frothy blood, meaning he had hit a lung. Dark red blood would have meant a heart shot. But alas, the arrow had struck a bit further back than he would have liked. It was still a good hit though, and the animal would surely die.

Then he sat down, watching the sun sink lower, and considered his options. He figured there were two hours of daylight left, and an Elk could last many hours with a pierced lung. The animal would bed down somewhere close and try to sleep his wound off. If Large Teeth came stumbling after him before he expired, then the elk would run hard and all-out, and Large Teeth might never find him again.

Large Teeth made his decision then. He would return tomorrow to track his kill.

LEVI SAT MOTIONLESS, HIDDEN AWAY IN A high pile of rocks set on an even higher ridge. He pulled the buffalo robe tight around him. It was quite warm, even if a bit damp from the rain the night before. On his back was a quiver of arrows, and on the rocks next to him, its corresponding bow. At his belt, a new tomahawk, or new to him at least, and the bone handled knife it had come paired with. He'd hobbled the old bag of bones in a small gulch some several hundred yards away. And next to it, he'd left his new horse, a fine, dapple-gray Blackfoot pony.

He'd ambushed its lone rider earlier that morning, when it was still dark out. The poor sod, wet and cold as he was, had been more concerned with bundling and rebundling his buffalo robe than paying attention to his surroundings. Now his hair decorated his own horse, and his robe warmed Levi, and his weapons might yet be used against his friends.

The last three hours had been quite entertaining, for Levi had just watched one of the Indians from the war party slink sideways across the landscape and lay a stalk on four elk. So focused was the Indian on the elk, he had remained oblivious to Levi watching him.

Making his shot, the Indian brave had hung around, checking the place where the elk had stood. And Levi, advantaged by his higher elevation, had watched as the small herd of animals made a run for a thick stand of cedar.

The brave had left after that, no doubt deciding to come back to track it in the morning, give it all night to expire and hope the wolves or a bear didn't find it first. For that's what Levi would do.

Indians were a funny lot, he thought then. Folks assigned them an occult sense of the natural world, and supranatural abilities. They assigned them a savagery in battle and a passion in love that was nothing more than an unfamiliar awe of their own dormant instincts. The truth of it was, they were the same. Silly, oblivious men, with petty dramas. They had no extra sense of nature, just more practice at it.

For Levi had always thought, place any man in the

wild long enough, and young enough, and a woodsmen he would be. Man was made for the wild places like a duck was water. The ways of wild things, the stories in the stars, the secrets paths of the land —for all to know, should they just listen.

Levi had listened, and he had learned. He'd adapted his ways to the Indian, taking the best they could teach and turning it towards his own ends. He had fashioned himself to their world that he might live in it. And they had tested each other, him and the Indian. And was not this, the ability to adapt to a new people, to thrive in any environment and lay claim upon life, was not this the highest test of a man?

He figured it so.

Then with night falling, and his Indian friend gone, Levi rose and started back towards his horses.

LARGE TEETH WOKE EARLY TO TRACK THE wounded elk. Strips of venison were already hanging above the lodge's small fire. He Who Shouts Loudly had killed a doe, and Red Horse a buck. If they found the elk today, they would have more than enough meat, probably too much, even with nine of them for the trip back.

Large Teeth briefly thought about not bothering to reclaim it, but he couldn't bring himself to leave the kill out there. It would be bad luck. The elk's spirit would tell the other elk what he had done, and they would hide themselves from him. No, he would go recover the kill, and they would use the meat as best they could.

"Nobody else wanted to go?" He Who Shouts Loudly asked.

“The others all take after Lazy One this morning,” Large Teeth replied.

He Who Shouts Loudly snickered.

Large Teeth led the way, and it took them very little time on horseback to reach the place where he'd made his shot.

Large Teeth pulled up on the reins and slipped off the back of the horse. He again found the blood trail, a little less obvious the morning after, and followed it a little way before losing it completely.

Then he worked circles around the area, carefully picking through dead leaves and scanning the grass. A little way ahead, He Who Shouts Loudly called, having regained the trail.

They tracked the wounded elk further, having to stop several times and circle an area to regain the trail. But it appeared after a while, that the bull had cut a straight line forward, not circling back or changing course, which made the trail easier to follow. It was a good sign too, for it meant the animal had been mortally wounded.

Eventually they lost the blood trail, but it did not matter, for they found elk tracks in the loose soil. And a little further on they found a place where the elk had made a mess of a steep embankment in their mad scramble up.

Large Teeth glanced towards the top of the ridge where he could just barely make out a patch of cedars tangled with pine. Heavy brush spilled over the top of the steep incline.

"It's a good place," Large Teeth said. "A safe place for him to bed."

He Who Shouts Loudly nodded.

They climbed to the top, winding their way around rocks and through the trees. Nothing stirred. No birds chirped. Death hung heavy in the place, but not a peaceful death. A haunted one, that made Large Teeth's blood run cold. He sensed it.

Then he saw it, and he froze, even as He Who Shouts Loudly cried out in fear.

The Elk had been transformed into a monster. Its skin and most of its muscles were missing and it stood on its hind legs. A knife was tied to one hoof, and a bloody scalp hung from the other. Two black eyes protruded from the beast's long white skull. Its antlers spread out above its head, tines red with blood, as if crowned by some great wickedness and set loose on them from the underworld.

Large Teeth scrambled backward, tripped over a log, and landed on his back. He was about to twist his body away in a mad attempt at escape, when he realized the monster had not moved after him. Slowly he stood up, and He Who Shouts Loudly crept up behind him, placing a nervous hand on his shoulder. They both moved closer to the hideous creature, bows held at the ready.

The beast was dead and had merely been butchered. Its remains raised on a wooden cross. It was a dark idol and Large Teeth had never seen such an evil thing.

Slowly, He Who Shouts Loudly ventured forward and inspected the scalp. A yellow ribbon was woven into the braids, and the two signature goose feathers decorated the end of it.

"It is Lazy One's hair," he said.

Large Teeth turned and ran.

LEVI HAD SLEPT THE DAY AWAY, HIDDEN away inside a small hollow, and rose from his restless slumber a few hours before sundown. Most of his night had involved butchering that poor Indian's elk and setting its carcass up as a scarecrow, which he chuckled about now. He'd made a mess of it, and wished he could see their reaction. They were a superstitious bunch, and he realized on that point, he did not have much room to talk. But with any luck, the elk would put a proper scare into them, and make them a bit more jumpy tonight.

He made his way over to a stand of trees then, and hacked into a fat looking cottonwood with his tomahawk opening a wide gash in the tree. He was lucky, for it had been warm all day, and the sap was not frozen. As the tree slowly bled, the sun sank a bit lower, even as the clouds in the North rose seemingly out of nowhere, pushing before them cold winds and a storm.

Levi rubbed the sap onto his hands and arms all the way up to his elbows, and then on his face. He applied it to any part of him that was exposed, and then to his clothes.

It was a trick Ol Mohe had taught him. The odor quieted horses, calmed them, and made them willing to follow strangers off. It was the sort of thing decent folk never bothered knowing, but was a thing known to Indians, miscreants, mountain men, and bushwhackers.

When he was done, he returned to the horses and set loose the old bag of bones. He had no use for the horse, and it would only slow him down.

Levi slapped the animal on the rump and watched as the horse charged off into the wild. He wondered where it would go and what it would do. If it would find some band of wild mustangs to follow, and if they would accept it as one of their own. It was gelded, which meant that it was the last of its line.

The thought saddened him, and he did not know why.

He had saved the buckskins taken off the brave he had killed, and these he cut into pieces. When he had four squares, he used them to wrap the dapple's hooves, tying them off with a cord of rawhide. The horse only fought him when he wrapped the hind hooves, but he held the horse steady, the way a farrier does when shoeing.

When he was done, the horse pranced nervously, somewhat spooked by the new feeling on his feet, but quieted down with a bit of steady soothing. The wraps would muffle the click of hooves on stone and let him ride a might quieter. The Blackfoot pony already had soft feet, and good instincts, so he figured the wraps might make him near invisible.

He climbed atop the dapple gray, repositioned the tomahawk on his belt. He wanted his guns back. He could shoot well enough with a bow, Ol Mohe had seen to that, but it had been years since he'd used one.

Then, suddenly curious, he took the bow in one hand, nocked an arrow, and fired it off at a tree no more than 15 paces away. The arrow flew past, missing the tree wholesale by more than a few inches and over a foot high off the knot he was aiming at.

He grunted in dismay, and flung another arrow, but had no better luck. Then he bent forward and patted the nervous horse. "Well, that's good to know, huh, boy." He cast the bow aside then, and unslung the arrows at his back, letting them fall to the earth.

He nudged the dapple forward beneath a gray and dying sky, lightning crackling in the distance.

Man and horse moved off through the trees, appearing as if a centaur, the horse wearing moccasins and the man draped in a great shaggy coat of Buffalo.

They moved silent as a shadow now, and night was falling.

⅄

IT BEGAN TO RAIN. LARGE TEETH WARMED himself at the fire. Across from him, He Who Shouts Loudly retold the story of what they had found. The others hung on his every word, faces contorted in fear.

"Naked bone, and strips of bloody mangled flesh, a red crown, and black eyes," He Who Shouts Loudly said.

"Enough," Large Teeth cried out. "It was meant to scare us. It is not evil."

"How can you say this?" He Who Shouts Loudly said. "You saw it too!"

"But what would do this?" Red Horse asked. "Only evil spirits."

"We should turn back," said Black Horn.

"Without Gray Wolf and Steals Many Horses?" Large Teeth asked. "And what about Apaniaki."

"This is different," Red Horse said. "The spirits are against it. Any man that believes the spirits are against him is not a coward, this has always been our way. No man can tell another to ignore the spirits or his dreams. This is our way."

"It is not a spirit," Large Teeth said. "It is a trick."

"A warning from Napi," Black Horn said. "Napi is trying to tell us to turn back."

He Who Shouts Loudly grunted at that, as if deep in thought, and sat back on his haunches.

"We wait for Gray Wolf," Red Horse said. "But then we leave."

The others agreed with him.

Large Teeth gritted his teeth and said nothing.

The others smoked their pipes tensely. The rain turned to ice outside and made clattering sounds on the outside of the lodge.

They had been so close, Large Teeth thought. He had been so close. He would lose Apaniaki forever, and Black Crow would not forgive them. They would say that he had brought the curse down on them by leaving the Elk out there in the night. They would shun him. They would not say it right away, but eventually, after the story had made its way around the fire many times. Such was the nature of stories told around fires. They stretched and morphed, filling in gaps and motivations as they grew.

Large Teeth stared at the dancing flames, and then he fed it more sticks. The storm raged harder outside.

"I will go check on the horses," Large Teeth said, adjusting the pistols in his belt. Then he pulled the Buffalo robe close around him, and took up the rifle.

He pushed through the heavy Buffalo hide they had used for a makeshift door and stumbled out into the blackness. It was sleeting and the frozen rain stung his cheeks and his hands, causing him to lose feeling. He walked forward towards the place where they had hobbled the horses.

When he did not find any sign of them, he ran forward, frantically searching the trees for any sign of them, thinking they'd moved further back into the trees to avoid the weather. Then lightning flashed, and all he saw during the brief moment of clear sight was an empty clearing and no horses whatsoever. Then he felt something underfoot. He picked it up. It was one of the rawhide hobbles.

Something moved behind him, and he heard the squidge of a foot in mud, and he was just turning—

LARGE TEETH CAME TOO INSIDE THE LODGE. The others stared at him, peering at him and whispering to each other. He felt very cold, and had been dreaming of an icy lake and drowning.

"The horses are gone," Black Horn said, holding out a piece of rawhide cordage, knotted on one side, and slashed on the other.

"The evil spirit stalks us," Red Horse said. "We heard commotion, and found it crouched over you, but it fled before taking your hair."

Large Teeth struggled to an elbow, and rubbed his pounding head. His hand came back with a streak of blood. Then feeling his waist, he realized that he no longer had the pistols. "Evil spirits do not try to scalp men. And they have no use for hair or guns. It was the Long Knife."

"What do we do now?" Black Horn cried out. "We have no horses, and Cold Maker has come?"

"You did this!" Red Horse shouted, pointing at Large Teeth. "You have brought this great evil down upon us. It has already killed Lazy One. Now it comes for us. It is not the Long Knife. No man does such things. Only an evil spirit."

"Large Teeth has done nothing wrong," He Who Shouts Loudly said. "We must wait for Gray Wolf and Steals Many Horses to return. Then we decide."

They sat silently after that but sleep visited no man. They stared at the fire, and they stared at each other. And they wondered what sort of demon had braved the storm and stole their horses.

Large Teeth's mind turned to Spotted Locust, to his murder and the lie he had told, and he grew very angry and scared, for surely he'd prompted this misfortune.

CHAPTER 14
THE SLAVE GIRL

Five days earlier...

THE MAN APANIAKI WOULD LATER COME TO learn was Charging Bull threw her from his horse. He was broad shouldered and lean. His nose was crooked and smashed as if it had been broken several times, but his jaw was still square. She fell from his horse, and the ground came up quick, smacking her in the face and testing the sturdiness of her wrist. She looked up to see him grinning, and she thought that he must surely be a demon. His face painted black and white, the white forming a triangle that covered his nose and mouth and chin.

She spat at him. He laughed.

The other Crow warriors scrambled to switch their buffalo hide saddles to the fresh mounts that they had just stolen. Charging Bull, the one that scooped her up, slid off the back of his horse and stripped it of its saddle.

Then he grabbed her up and with a rawhide cord, lashed her hands together in front of her. He pulled another mount near and set her on it the way one might set a toddler on his first pony.

After he'd saddled and mounted a fresh horse, they were off again, racing across the plains beneath a white moon. He did not give her the reins, but instead held the lead of her horse as it trailed behind his.

Apaniaki bent forward holding on to the horse's mane as best she could with both hands tied together, and she gripped its sides with her legs until she thought they would surely give out. It was an awful way to ride a horse.

They rode all night and then on into the day, only stopping to switch mounts. The braves ate in the saddle, taking little handfuls of dried meat and berries from the leather pouches at their belts. None was offered to her.

Then night found them again, just as the land transitioned from hills to plains. Apaniaki had longed for night to come, had longed for her feet to touch the ground, and had longed to disappear from the waking world. Night had surely meant sleep. But when the sun set, the moon rose, and the men had kept riding forward, and seemed to not care about sleep or breaks.

This caused her great consternation, for she felt near to breaking from exhaustion, and yet, these men moved on through the night, drawing from a deep well of stamina that she could barely fathom.

Sleep did come to her, eventually, but it was ridiculously short effort, for she woke up rolling on the ground, the earth once more having reached up to smack her. Hooves passed over her head, and she was suddenly dragged screaming back to reality by the fear of being trampled.

And once again, Charging Bull stood over her.

He gave her a drink from his waterskin. It tasted stale and almost putrid, but she swallowed, thankful for the chance to soothe her aching throat. Then he fed her a handful of pemmican which she scarfed out of his hand as if his dog or horse.

Hours earlier she would have never let herself be so humiliated, now she gave it no thought. The food left her only more thirsty, but Charging Bull had already stood and put away the waterskin, and she was afraid to ask for more. He bent over, picked her up again, and sat her on the back of the horse.

They rode on.

There was a logic to not feeding her, and to keeping her thirsty. It wasn't all malice she intuited. A thirsty prisoner can't run very far, a weak and hungry one can run even less.

The next time she fell from the horse, she was not set on it upright, but thrown over crossways on her belly and lashed onto the animal the way one would lash a dead deer across its back. Here, she felt every bounce and jostle of the horse and soon her abdomen ached from bracing against the horse's bounce. She decided then that given the chance, she would not fall from the horse again.

That chance came when night fell on the third day, and Charging Bull untied her from the horse and let her fall slack to the ground. They stopped and ate and smoked, and then they slept for three hours, rising while the night was still very young.

Charging Bull was about to throw her across her horse like a dead deer once more, but she protested, kicking at him with her feet. Then she scrambled onto the horse, before he could recover.

He laughed at that, and nodded, before saying something to the others that she couldn't understand. Then they laughed, and she stuck her hands out to him indignantly. He seemed to think for a second, and then took his knife, and grabbing her hands roughly, snatched them towards him, where he slashed her bindings.

"If you run, I kill," he signed to her.

She nodded in agreement. Then he made her ride ahead of him.

The following day, the mountains rose mightily before them, and the land transitioned from flat grassy lands to hills spotted with trees and large rocks. By night the hills gave way to mountain trails, and as they wound their way higher, the prairie fell away below them, awash in the pearl luminescence of the moon, and the wind rattled through dying trees, making a lonely, peaceful melody that Apaniaki thought to be the sound of melancholy itself.

As morning broke, they started to descend into a valley, and far in the distance, Apaniaki picked out the small fingers of smoke that signaled cookfires, and then ever so briefly she spotted the white triangles that were the Crow lodges. The trail hooked right, taking them suddenly lower.

Her horse struggled to keep its footing on the loose shale, but she guided him coolly, her heart pounding in her breast, and when she looked up, having finally reached the bottom, Charging Bull stared at her.

He had seen her fear, and he started to laugh, and so she laughed. She laughed with sudden relief, and then she turned red, and remembered her anger, and Charging Bull looked even more amused.

When they reached the Crow camp, the women and children crowded around, running and jumping in excitement as the warriors bellowed triumphant war cry's. Some of the women began to wail, and Apaniaki assumed it was because they did not see their sons, or brothers, or husbands among the returning men. She felt for them, despite herself, for it was a feeling she herself knew.

CHARGING BULL LED HER TO HIS LODGE. Raven Wing stood outside, arms folded, her face contorted with rage, even as her eyes sparked.

Charging Bull motioned for her to sit, and so Apaniaki sat down in the dirt. Then she watched as he disappeared inside the lodge. His black-haired wife shot Apaniaki a venomous glare. She had dark, stormy eyes, high cheekbones, and a delicate nose, all underlined by thin lips and set to a harsh countenance. The woman whirled, throwing open the flap of the teepee and following her man inside.

A yellow dog drew near to Apaniaki, growling at first. She held out the back of her hand and let the dog sniff it. Slowly, he accepted her presence, then he let her pet him.

The arguing continued from inside the teepee. The stern voice of Charging Bull followed by the wife's long emotional rants, rising in pitch and fervor. The dog put his head in Apaniaki's lap.

After a while, all went silent in the teepee, and then Apaniaki heard the sounds of love making, and bile tickled the back of her throat. The yellow dog looked sadly into her eyes.

SHE WAS PUT TO WORK AFTER THAT AND LEFT unmolested by Charging Bull. He had apparently lost the argument, and Apaniaki was glad for it. She was their slave, and Apaniaki had thought at first that it would stay that way.

But a day later, the first visitor came. Charging Bull hauled her out of the teepee, pulling her from her work tanning the Buffalo hides and forced her down onto her knees by kicking the back of them.

Before her stood a proud-looking brave. He was shorter than Charging Bull, his face leathern, but still youthful. He wore a necklace of grizzly claws, and a fine coat made of otter. He had brought two horses which stood nearby—one a pretty looking blue roan with a black mane, and the other a red paint pony with a large splotch over his eye. They looked fine enough, and Apaniaki was positive that she was to become this brave's wife.

But Charging Bull and the brave haggled for a while, and then the brave wandered off, his head hanging, and Charging Bull disappeared back into the teepee.

She heard more arguing after that.

APANIAKI LAY WIDE AWAKE THAT NIGHT. THE wind howled outside, and the patter of the rain on the hide walls soothed her. Coldmaker had come. It was only a matter of time before the first snow would follow. She worried then about her rescue.

She thought of Black Crow and Large Teeth, and the stranger that she had freed. She wondered if even now Black Crow rode to rescue her, or even Large Teeth. If she was married off, she would be no use to him, no use to anyone in her tribe, even if they got her back. No brave wanted another man's woman. Not after he had left his mark on her, and surely not one stained by the touch of the enemy.

Or maybe they would not come. She wondered then, if she was worth it to the men it would take to steal her back. Black Crow would surely want to, for she was his daughter, but could he convince the others? The tribe loved and respected him, but she was only a girl.

Large Teeth would surely come. She knew it.

Her thoughts turned to the bearded stranger with the kind eyes and the hairy chest. The bold one that had dared invade her father's lodge. She wondered what had become of him. She wondered at the flush that even now colored her cheeks in the darkness, and the flutter in her chest as she remembered being found naked by the lake. It was a strange feeling. One that scared her and felt all the more cruel and foolish for the absurdity of it. But maybe that was it, maybe she allowed herself these feelings for that very reason. The simple fact that it would never happen.

THE NEXT DAY, A NEW BUYER ARRIVED. THIS man was older and had a scar that cut across his face from the tip of his jaw to the opposite corner of his forehead. His eyes were dark and unfeeling. He had the eyes of a wolf, not a man, and Apaniaki's blood ran cold at the sight of him. It turned to ice upon seeing the four horses he had brought, one of which was a fine black stud.

Charging Bull and the man negotiated, and for a second, her heart caught in her throat as Charging Bull considered the man's offer. But at last he was sent off.

The argument from the teepee was even louder this time, and the sounds of love making that followed more vigorous.

Again, Apaniaki stared into the yellow dog's sad eyes.

After that, she was sent to fetch water and Raven Wing showed her the way to the river, which ran along the far edge of the camp. Between camp and the river, they passed by a herd of horses. Apaniaki took note of where the Crow warriors sat. If she was to escape, she would need a horse.

There seemed to be only two warriors that watched them. They lounged on a log at the edge of camp, snickering to each other as they worked making arrows.

At the river, Raven Wing cuffed her behind the ears and told her to fill the water sacks. Apaniaki filled them dutifully. She took no action against the abuse, but showed no pain either.

When they passed back through the camp, her heart jumped at the sight of a bearded man, and then dropped at the realization that he was different. There were two bearded men, sitting outside separate teepees. Their women working dutifully beside them. Crow women. Apaniaki found it odd that the Crow let the two Long Knives live with them. Live alongside them. The Blackfoot would never allow such a thing.

⤴

THE NEXT MORNING, SHE STOLE THE KNIFE. When Raven Wing left the teepee, Apaniaki grabbed it. She hiked up her buckskin dress and lashed it firmly to her thigh with a piece of rawhide cord.

When the wife returned, she put Apaniaki back to work on the buffalo hides but did not notice the missing knife. They were almost finished with them, and Apaniaki wondered what task she would be set upon next.

Even as Raven Wing hurled abuses and slapped her with a cupped hand, she kept quiet and silently thanked her, for her jealousy had saved her from promotion to wife.

She noted the comings and goings of the Crow braves on the edge of camp. The trails they kept to as they walked the perimeter.

She had not yet decided if she could steal a horse. It seemed she needed to, but it would be dangerous, and she knew she could not fight off one of the scouts if she was caught.

The next morning no new suitor arrived, and as the day dragged on, she became more and more sure that she had survived the day as a slave and not a Crow squaw.

But would she be so lucky tomorrow? Or the day after? Would not Charging Bull grow wearisome of his wife's ire?

She could wait no longer. It had to be tonight, she decided. She could not risk having a brave show up tomorrow with the right number of horses. Or worse, Charging Bull reopening negotiations with the wolfish man and his cruel eyes.

She had to escape, had to make it back to her tribe, had to make it back to her old life, even if that meant back to Large Teeth. And she would be thankful for him this time. She could make a life with Large Teeth if this was the alternative.

She thought of her foolishness that night by the lake, when she had prayed to the Great One that the wedding might be averted. She wondered even now if she had brought this on herself. "Careful what you ask the Spirits," Red Beaver used to say. "They do not always answer the way we expect."

She finished kneading the brains into her hide, and then Raven Wing struck her again, just for good measure, and motioned for her to hang them up. Then the woman threw empty waterskins at her and motioned for her to go.

Apaniaki gathered up the waterskins and made her way to the river just outside of camp. The sun was just beginning to set, and as it fell, she wished it along. She prayed that night and with it her escape, would hurry along.

With the waterskins filled, she started back. Several braves, lounging outside a teepee cooed at her and laughed. She ignored them. The yellow dog met her outside the lodge, and she stopped, water sloshing, to pet it.

She wondered if the yellow dog would like to come with her when she left.

Inside, she hung the waterskins up, and then attempted to help Raven Wing prepare the food. The woman shooed her away and motioned for her to sit back in her corner.

Apaniaki sat and watched the woman work.

In a way, Apaniaki felt sorry for her. Her husband had dragged another woman back and tried to keep her. Apaniaki would probably beat her senseless too if she'd been in the woman's place. She twirled a buckskin fringe around her finger and tried to make her presence as small as possible, giving little furtive glances around the teepee. She tried to never look too proud, for that was sure to draw the woman's anger, but she never showed pain or consternation either, for that seemed to draw even more abuse. So, she just sat. Sat as small as possible and considered her escape.

When they laid down for sleep, and she heard Charging Bull's snoring, and Raven Wings slow breathing, she would take the knife and slice a hole in the teepees wall close to the ground. She would slip outside, as quietly as possible, taking with her one of the freshly tanned buffalo robes.

Then she would head straight away to the edge of camp, and slip around on the outskirts to where they kept the horses.

She figured if she could get to the far edge, she could lure a horse to the trees. Then she would be gone.

If she couldn't get a horse, then she would have to leave on foot. The thought of that scared her. It was hundreds of miles back to her people's home, and Cold Maker was coming. She would surely die on that journey. But death, she decided, would be better than dishonor, far better than being a Crow squaw.

CHARGING BULL'S ENTRANCE SHOOK HER from her plans and her thoughts. He glanced around, as if looking for something, and then spotting her, his gaze settled.

Raven Wing, for the first time since her arrival, smiled at her, and Apaniaki knew. She knew that she was too late. That she had waited too long. That the lack of a suitor earlier that day had been a terrible sign. A lump grew in the back of her throat.

"Come," Charging Bull said.

Slowly, she rose. The blood rushed to her head, making her dizzy with fear. Her chest compressed, and her empty stomach burned with acid.

He grabbed her arm and hauled her the rest of the way up, then shoved her forward towards the teepee's flap.

"No," she said, resisting his pull. But Raven Wing

walloped her on the back of the head, and she felt her feet, absent of her own will, take two tiny steps forward.

Then she was outside.

Her buyer stood in silhouette, a fiery orange sky behind him. He was large, his shoulders made even broader by the shaggy buffalo robe draped across them. He was all dark fur and shaggy hide, a beast, surely.

And then she saw the long string of horses standing quietly nearby. Ten of them including his. She counted them again just to be sure. Charging Bull shoved her forward, and she stumbled, falling hard on her knees before the figure.

She didn't dare look up at him, lest the nightmare become real. Lest she provoke him into following through with his purchase. But she already knew that was foolishness.

She side-eyed the horses grazing peacefully next to her. Ten whole horses, for her? Charging Bull had certainly got his price. There was a perverse gladness in her heart—that she should bring such a price. A brief flash of pride that confused her.

Gentle hands helped her up, even as she tensed her body, still not daring to look her buyer in the face. But the hands lifted her chin, daring her to accept this new fate, and then, helpless as she was against her own morbid curiosity, she nearly fainted in recognition.

It was the stranger. The one from that day at the lake, with his dark beard, and piercing eyes. It was the Long Knife.

He lifted a finger to his lips to quiet her, the same way he had at the lake.

Charging Bull gathered up the leads of the horses.

And the stranger, the one that rode with Napi, helped her up onto a little black mare.

He then threw himself onto a second horse; a big red horse with white socks and a star on its forehead. She gave a tiny gasp. It was Star Runner, Large Teeth's horse. Her mind raced through a thousand different possibilities and came up with none that made sense. None that led to the stranger riding Star Runner.

The man glanced at her, his eyes soft, but his mouth set sternly, and he gave her a small nod that told her to follow.

Then he nudged Star Runner forward, and she followed, somewhat peeved by her own willingness.

CHAPTER 15
THE BLIZZARD

THEY MADE CAMP IN A HIGH MOUNTAIN PASS on the opposite end of the valley. It was a hidden place, set back in a cove of trees. Levi dug two holes, right next to each other, which took some time as the ground was frozen.

The girl watched him work.

"Gather wood," Levi signed to her.

She wandered off, and a little time later, reappeared with bundles of wood for the fire. Two trips later, and he signed for her to stop.

He then started a fire using a small bit of the gunpowder he'd traded off Tanglefoot back at the Crow camp. He'd managed to get a horn of powder and a sack of shot from him too. He was glad to have his pistols back, and the Hawken, having taken them off of the leader of the war party. And at least now he didn't feel so naked.

He retrieved some of the elk meat from the pack on his horse and started slicing it into small chunks. Then he placed them on a sharp stick and set them to cook over the fire.

The girl motioned towards his horse, and then signed, "where from?"

Levi signed back; I stole it.

Is he dead? the girl signed.

No, Levi signed. Then he thumped his chest, signaling his own displeasure at the fact.

The girl's brow furled, and Levi wondered what he said wrong.

He handed her a piece of elk meat, one of the smaller pieces close to being done. She took it from him and scarfed it down. He handed her more of the elk, and she kept it up. He saved the last two chunks for himself.

After a while, as the fire burned lower, he pointed back to his horse then and asked her how she knew its former rider.

She signed back that he wanted her for a wife. Then she signed that the horse's name was Star Runner. Then she returned to scarfing down the elk.

He thought about that for a while, and decided he'd keep the name.

There was a rustle out in the dark, feet on leaves. Levi's head snapped up, and his hand found the rifle. He spun in the direction of the noise.

But it was only Loki.

Apaniaki gave a small gasp, and the Coyote gave her a little growl. What Levi recognized as a love growl, at least. He signed to her that it was fine. Then taking the last piece of elk off the spit, he cut a portion of it off and tossed it to the dog. Loki snapped it up and inhaled it.

"Damn dog, don't even enjoy it."

Apaniaki watched Napi circle around the fire, completely fearless, and then curl up next to the stranger that had rescued her... bought her. She hadn't decided what he'd done yet, or how she felt about it. Actually, she had, and she was glad for it.

Her head was swimming with relief at no longer belonging to the Crows, and trepidation at this stranger's intentions. At this weird man, draped in hides, his face covered in hair, who made friends with Napi, both creator and trickster.

She still felt the electric charge that she had that day at the Lake, and she still did not know what had compelled her to set him loose that night the Crow had attacked. There was the idea of him, as the tall stranger come to save her from her life, and the reality she now sat across from. A reality she had no real knowledge of.

The man petted the animal, and it bristled at his touch, its little growls like purrs, with one long low growl that was easy to interpret as displeasure, except for the fact that it did not move away from him. She had not seen Napi the day he had come into camp, but all the others had talked about it. Napi had defended the man, listened and obeyed him. They had feared what to do with him after that.

She pulled the buffalo robe tighter around her shoulders, helping to shield her against the cold wind blowing down off the mountain.

As if on cue, the stranger poked the fires, exposing red hot coals. He buried them then, using the same dirt that had come from the holes.

In the darkness, she could barely make out his movements, but then she felt him come close, and she smelled him. He smelled musky, but not dirty, like cottonwoods and earth. She tensed as he grabbed her arm, and she started to pull away from him, but then he shushed her, the way one soothes a horse, or some wild and lonely thing. She felt hot breath on her cheek, and her body moved into him even as her mind told her to stop.

And then he moved her towards the place where the second fire had been buried, guiding her through the darkness with a firm hand.

He made his bed over the first hole filled with coals and covered with dirt, and then patted the earth covering the coals of the second, and she laid down, wrapping herself up in the heavy buffalo robe. She felt the heat emanating from the coals buried beneath her and they felt good.

She woke early in the morning, deeply chilled, her feet numb, and her cheeks and nose bitten by Cold Maker. The man was already up, moving about the horses. She lay still, not wanting to move. Stiff, and cold.

It was dark out. Too dark to travel, and since it was cloudy, she could not see the stars, nor the moon. The man restarted the fire, and they warmed themselves by it while waiting for the sky to lighten.

When the sky turned from black to gray, he gathered her up and placed her on the horse. He didn't ask, nor coax, he simply did it. Simply packed her up onto the horse the way one would a bundle of sticks, or a bale of furs, or any other precious possession. Or even one not so precious, but his, nonetheless.

THEY RODE ALL DAY, DEEPER INTO THE mountains, and in the opposite direction of her people. At noon, they stopped on a high ridge. He gave her a handful of dried meat, and below them, the trees swayed mightily, shaking beneath Cold Maker's breath. She watched them shimmer and sway.

She signed to him then, asking where they were going.

He signed back, that it was a place that belonged to him.

Apaniaki wondered if she should try to leave him. Try to escape back to her people. She had a horse now, and she still had the knife that she'd stolen from Charging Bull's lodge.

She felt it pressed against her thigh.

They continued like this for several days. Camping at night, huddling around the fire, and making their bed atop the coals. In the morning they would wake to gray skies, and the brooding of Cold Maker. Sun Boy remained hidden.

On the fourth day, Cold Maker brought the first few flakes of winter, and Levi hurried her onto the horse. It snowed all day. Thick and wet, and melting nearly as soon as it touched them. By midday she was soaked, and shivering, and her feet and hands were completely numb. The land had turned white, and the trees bent under the weight of the snow and ice. Steam rose from the horses, and the melted snow made icicles on their manes.

The man kept checking a small round object, the color of a brass button. He was following it. Asking it to lead them. Or at least that is what she surmised.

The man had grown concerned. She could read it in him. He was cold, and something had made him weak. His face was ashy.

As the storm grew more forceful, they lost visibility, and the snow piled into giant drifts. And then it appeared, seemingly out of nowhere. A structure made of firm logs and covered in snow. And another structure, set somewhat back from it, with a pole corral. Apaniaki knew it immediately to be the place that belonged to him.

He slid off the back of Star Runner, the wind whipping at his furs, ice in his beard. He pulled her down off the back of the horse, and then guided her to the door. He kicked away the snow that had blown up around the bottom of it, then he unbarred it, and tried to open it, but ice had frozen it shut. Then he put his shoulder into it, and after three massive heaves and a grunt he fell inside.

He left her there and went to put away the horses.

She looked around. It was small, and cold, but a firm shelter. It felt good to be out of the wind. There was a small table in the middle, and a single chair. In another corner was a bed, made up of furs, and buffalo blankets. On the floor, a giant grizzly stared up at her, having been made into a rug.

The walls were lined with steel traps. She had seen them before, once before when the Long Knives from the North had come and traded with them. Black Crow had traded for three of the traps.

When Levi returned, he started a fire in the stone box, and soon the small wooden lodge was full of warmth. Apaniaki sat near the fire. The man shrugged out of his heavy coat and spread it near the fire to dry.

Then from a high shelf, he retrieved a jug. Uncorked it and took a swig. Apaniaki watched as he grimaced. He was in pain.

She rose then and unbuttoned his shirt, to reveal the same poultice she had put on his shoulder many sleeps earlier. It was infected. She put a hand on his forehead. He was burning up.

He took another swig from the jug.

This is why you brought me here? she signed to him.

No, he signed back, then he again explained to her that he had been cursed by an evil spirit. That he had slept in the place of the dead.

She didn't know what to make of that. This curse he had signed of. What she did know was that the shoulder would kill him if she didn't tend to it.

She placed the water skins he'd brought inside by the fire to thaw. They were frozen and swollen, and she was surprised they had not burst. Then she helped him shrug out of his buckskin shirt and guided him to the bed of furs.

He fell asleep almost instantly.

When the waterskins were thawed, she sat down next to him. She cleaned out the wound, and he muttered in his sleep, his forehead beaded in sweat. From her medicine bag, she made a tea of dried boneset.

His eyes fluttered open, and she held the cup of tea to his lips, making him drink all of it down. With any luck it would help his fever.

He was lucky that she'd caught the shoulder so early. A few days more and it would have likely killed him. With any help from the Great One, he would make it through.

Then she let him sleep. After a while, she made a stew of the elk bones, and woke him once more, making him drink down the broth.

His fever was still high, and so she cooled him with a piece of buckskin dipped in a pan of water. This continued late into the night, and outside the wind howled louder. As she tended to him, she studied his face. The deep lines cut by the sun; his wind kissed lips, and the curls of hair that carpeted a big barrel chest.

He had bought her to heal him. There was relief in the knowledge, and the slightest pang of hurt. Eight horses, she thought. She didn't know why she was upset. Yet still she was mad. She sat down in the bed next to him and continued to cool his brow with the water and the buckskin. She looked around the little cabin and listened to the storm outside. It was so peaceful, warm, and safe.

The safest she'd felt in a long time, and she was upset. A smile fluttered across her lips, even as a tear traced its way down her cheek. She looked back at the man, his face twisted in fever.

WHEN LEVI WOKE, HE DID NOT KNOW WHERE he was. He was shivering, and still tired, and felt weak. He pushed himself up in bed and looked down next to him. The girl was there. Sleeping peacefully beside him. His pain was replaced by a small peace, and an unfamiliar comfort as he realized the girl had tended him through the night.

He reached out a hand and brushed a few wayward strands of hair back from her bronze forehead. Then she was up, swift as a desert rattler.

He felt the blade beneath his chin, and for a second there was no recognition in her eyes, still clouded as they were by dream. He stared into them, her pale grey eyes and watched as recognition replaced confusion.

Slowly, he wrapped his hand around hers, the one that held the wavering blade beneath his chin. He felt her arm, tensed for action, surrender beneath his grip. He peeled the blade from loose fingers. He watched her eyes, soften. And he saw her as he had the very first time, doe eyed and slightly frightened.

Her lips were pink, apart just slightly, as if searching for the thing to say, and then he pulled her close. He kissed her.

Her lips felt good, and the kiss was returned for but a second, and then she pulled away from him abruptly. He reached for her, but she had already slipped backwards. She stood flattening her dress, flustered, and unwilling to look at him.

He glanced at the blade in his hands, the one that had been held beneath his chin. Then he shifted his gaze back at to the woman before him, studied the gentle round of her shoulders, the animal grace in her hips, and the small quickness coiled in her legs as she paced the cabin like a caged lion.

She wasn't frightened, but rather upset. And he struggled to understand why, or what if anything he had done wrong.

Then, as if making up her mind about something, she caught up the great buffalo blanket that lay by the fire, wrapped it around her shoulders, and left the cabin, closing the door hard behind her.

Levi dropped back down into the bed of furs, too weak and confused to chase after her.

CHAPTER 16
HOT SPRINGS

SHE STOOD IN FRONT OF HIM SHIVERING, her hair wet from her walk. Snowflakes having fallen from the trees outside now clung to her black hair like so many stars. Her cheeks and nose were rosy with cold. She looked worried, but her jaw was set in that determined sort of way.

Take me back to my people, she signed.

"We're snowed in here," Levi signed back. He pushed himself up in the bed, and swung dead legs over the edge.

"I don't care," she signed back.

"Need you to lift the curse first," he signed.

She huffed at that, turning away from him and marching back towards the fire. She started prodding and poking it, this time more vigorously than the last. Theatrically even, as if it wasn't already going strong.

Levi was unsure what he'd said, or what he'd done to upset her, but it began to dawn on him that she was perhaps sick of getting kidnapped. He tried to push himself up onto his feet, but his shoulder sang in pain. Gasping, he steadied himself.

She rushed over and steadied him with a hand, her face concerned. He sat back down heavily, and she examined the wrapping she'd applied the night before. Then removed it and cleaned his wound, silently. He studied her as she worked, but she ignored him. Occasionally, she was more rough than he felt reasonable, and he let her know it with a hard grunt.

When she was done, he signed, "Thank you."

She stepped in front of him, and then signed quickly and harshly, "Worth ten horses?".

He laughed then, not know what she was on about, and her face flushed at his laugh. She stomped off.

THE SNOW WAS DEEP AND WOULD HAVE COME up to his knees, but the snowshoes kept him on top of it. Seeing just how much it had snowed; he wasn't quite sure exactly how they'd managed to make it to the cabin. They'd been lucky. Lucky they were so close when the blizzard really set to it, and lucky the trail was so navigable as the last half of it followed right along a cliff face. But still, it was quite a miracle. There'd be no getting out of here for a while, at least not on horseback. With snowshoes on a man could get along alright, but they wouldn't take a body very far.

It was only while brushing down the horses that he realized he didn't know her name. He'd just taken to thinking of her as the girl, or the woman with blue eyes, or the medicine woman, and he felt somewhat foolish then. As she likely thought him a lout, snatching her up as he did, and dragging her off into the mountains, without even giving her so much as a "what is your name?" Shit, he even knew the horse's name. At this point she didn't know him from Adam, and although he considered what he'd done to be about the closest thing to rescuing, he could see how things might look different from her end.

He fed the horses mesquite beans that he'd stored in the loft two summers earlier, and took stock of their situation. He didn't have much feed, about a month's worth of the beans. They were a serviceable enough feed replacement when one didn't have grain, which was pretty much all the time out here. He'd need to turn them loose so they could find grass, and the sooner the better so he could save the beans. They would paw up the snow to get at the grass. And he'd have to try to get them through the small pass that led to a little glen. The glen was large enough to winter a couple of horses, but likely no more'n three, and if when the going got really rough, as it would in another couple months, he could bark a cottonwood from the lake if they ran out of the beans. The horses, especially these Indian ponies, would eat cottonwood bark if the starving got bad enough.

He'd chosen this place for its wintering abilities. High enough up that the Indians weren't likely to poke around, but with access to passable forage, a lake full of beaver somewhat close, and plenty of game about. That wasn't to say it couldn't get dicey, but winters in the mountains were always hard. But they would make it. There was game enough, and they had enough of the elk left to last a while. Beaver tail would keep em in fat all winter. Keep em from starving.

Men had starved in the mountains, simply by not knowing the right way of things. He'd heard tale of a man that killed a big bull moose, which kept him in meat almost all winter, springtime came, and he was skin and bones. Another trapper found him, right there on death's door with a whole hindquarter of the moose still hanging in the smokehouse. Moose was too lean, and he'd starved himself with a full belly.

APANIAKI RAN HER HANDS THROUGH HER hair—stringy and greasy. She realized then, just how much she missed bathing. Picking up the bucket next to the door, she ventured outside to gather snow.

She melted the bucket full of snow by the fire and took a rag, which was really just an old cotton shirt, to use as sponge. Peeling off her buckskin dress, she dipped one toe tentatively into the bucket. It had been weeks since her last bath, and the grime came off easily. Yet, she still cringed at the chilled water.

As she cleaned, her thoughts returned to the Long Knife. They'd slept next to each other, and she was glad for it. And she had wanted him to kiss her. But it could not be? She was a Piikani, and he was a Long Knife. Her people would never allow it. Her father would never allow it...

But even as she thought this, she realized it was but a small excuse to hide a greater fear. When she lifted his curse, or chased away the evil spirits, would he not simply leave? Why keep her? The thought snatched her up and dumped her right on her head.

She had just started on the other leg, when the door opened.

It was the Long Knife.

He stopped and stared, turned beet red, stammered, and then turned right back around and closed the door.

She giggled as he hurried back out the door.

She finished her towel bath after that, and Levi

returned about an hour later carrying a bundle of willow branches under one arm. He greeted her warmly and said nothing about his sudden departure. Then he placed the bundle of sticks near the fire and signed to her that they needed to thaw.

WHAT IS YOUR NAME? LEVI SIGNED.

The girl's face softened, and he caught just the flicker of a smile. She signed back Butterfly Woman, and then said, "Apaniaki" in her own tongue.

"Butterfly Woman," Levi said, half to himself, and half to her.

And yours? she signed back.

"Levi," he said.

She repeated it back, "Le-Vi."

He laughed, and she blushed. He hadn't meant to embarrass her, and he felt badly about it. He realized then that this woman, this tough as nails woman, who'd followed him through the mountains, braved a Crow raid, and weathered snowstorms was just that—a woman. A delicate, sensitive, and fickle creature who blushed when he laughed thoughtlessly. There was a certain responsibility in that, one that he'd not been prepared to have heaped upon him.

"What is wrong?" Apaniaki signed.

"Nothing," he signed back. Then he said that he would call her, "Bright Eyes," and he signed it back to her, and she smiled in a way that lit the inside of the cabin all up.

He'd not ever met an Indian with colored eyes, but he'd heard tales of it. Some could be accounted for as the offspring of earlier frontiersmen, for many an indentured man had ran off and joined up with a tribe in the time of the colonies. And many a trader had wintered in the hut of a pretty Indian girl.

But he'd also met a Spaniard once, an educated and well-read man, who he'd spent a few weeks with down Louisiana way. The Spaniard had talked about a Welsh prince named Madoc who had discovered America far before Columbus. Legend had it that Madoc and his crew had even started a settlement, and then at some point joined with or became the Mandan. "Many of the Mandan are peculiar in way and appearance, resembling a white man more than anything else," the Spaniard had said. "Blue or green eyes. Sometimes blonde and brown hair."

Regardless, the Spaniard was loathe to answer questions or share more details. And it wasn't until he got stone drunk one night, that he told Levi how he'd come to know of this, saying that his grandfather, when just a young Spanish officer, had helped kill a party of French explorers. The Frenchmen had managed to find definitive proof of Welsh settlement. But when Levi had asked him what the proof was, the Spaniard had merely laughed, and said he did not know, because the Spanish Army had destroyed whatever this evidence was, fearing that it might make England even more boisterous in her territorial claims.

Apaniaki touched his arm then and signed, "Where are you from?"

And he told her, as best he could using sign, of the mountains far to the east, and the curious mountain folk, his folk, that had settled them. They swapped stories after that, which was difficult, and confusing, for sign language was utterly practical, built as it was for trade, and war, and making peace, not the telling of histories. And occasionally they taught each other a word. And when there came a place where language failed, whether of the tongue, or the hand; they spoke the language of the heart, using a smile, or a frown, a darting of the eyes, a quick flash of the wrist, a twirling of the hair, or a deep weeping laugh conjured up from the pits of their bellies.

At one point, Apaniaki leaned forward, and Levi felt the sudden urge to try to try and kiss her again, to pull her close. But her withdrawal earlier still hung heavy in his mind, and he hesitated.

She reached up, fingers searching his collar, and finding the necklace. The chain made of silver, and strung along the bottom was the family crest, a shield with the image of a wolf. It was an old family heirloom. He had asked his father about the wolf once, and he had said it was Skoll, who chased the moon across the sky.

"What is this?" she signed.

"My mother's," Levi signed back.

"She was of the People?" Apaniaki signed.

"No," Levi said. "She was a Dane." Even though the words meant nothing to her, or to him even. For he had given little thought to where his people had come from. He was of the Great Smoky Mountains.

Apaniaki nodded and said a word he couldn't understand.

"She died," Levi said, "while having me."

The woman's face clouded with sympathy.

"It is what it is," Levi signed.

She nodded back, understanding in her eyes.

"And your father?" the woman asked.

Levi stared at the fire, and across from him, sat his father. Slumped in his Planter's chair the way he'd sat most of Levi's brief childhood. A jug of corn whiskey next to him. He'd been about 10 years old as he figured it, and it was blowing cold outside. Snowing. He walked the ten miles it took to reach Ol' Mohe's cabin. Ol' Mohe was a Cherokee, who sometimes came around to break horses for his father. He was no relation, and less a friend to his father than an acquaintance, but he'd taken a liking to Levi. He'd showed him how to tame horses, how to check their health. On occasion, after a long day of work, and when his father had not yet returned from a day of drinking, Ol' Mohe would take him hunting, and teach him the names of things, and show him the ways of moving silently in the woods—

"You were born under a dark star is what he used to say," Levi said. "I left when I was ten or so," Levi signed, narrating all the while. "Ol' Mohe raised me up the rest of the way. Taught me how to hunt, how to track, how to build a fire the old way. Showed me how to move quietly in the woods. Even taught me what it meant to count coup on a man."

"What happened to him?" Apaniaki asked.

"He died," Levi signed. "Or was murdered."

"Who did it," Apaniaki asked.

"Don't know," Levi signed. Then he stumbled through the story, not sure how much translated through his motions, telling her how they found him thrown off the side of a trace. His head bashed in. And how Levi had headed west after that, and didn't look back. And how he worked on a keelboat until he had enough to start trapping.

She leaned forward then, a tenderness in her eyes, and they both stayed quiet. Then she said, "dark star," and signed it to make sure she was saying it right.

"I call you, Dark Star," Apaniaki said, smiling gently.

"A name for a name," Levi said back. "Somehow don't sound like a bad thing when you say it."

"Is this the curse you come for?" she signed.

"No," he said. Then he reminded her of the Ute's attack, and how they'd stolen his horses and shot him in the shoulder. He spoke of taking shelter in the burial grounds, and how afterwards, he'd lost his horse again, and the whistling in the night.

"You are not of the people. Our spirits are not your spirits," she signed. "I do not believe these spirits follow you."

"Am I not cursed?" he asked.

"Do you dream?" she signed.

"Not really." He shrugged.

"Other bad spirits have been with you for a long time," Apaniaki signed.

"Suppose running from a dark star ain't really all that possible," Levi said, more to himself than her, for he didn't bother trying to sign. "When you look up again the dark star is still right there, up above, shining down."

"I will bring you dreams again," Apaniaki signed to him.

They said nothing after that. The two of them, watching the fire burn low. After a while, she fell asleep, her head on his shoulder and he scooped her up in his arms and laid her in the great bed of furs, then retreated to the floor in front of the hearth.

THE NEXT MORNING, APANIAKI WOKE TO find herself alone. Le-Vi was gone. She missed him. Last night had been the first time in a long time that she had truly laughed, she thought. The cabin should have felt like a prison. A little wooden prison, surrounded by a moat of snow, and a fence made of mountains, but it never felt like that when he was here. Instead, it felt like the only truly free place on earth. Free of worry, free of fear, and free of death.

Levi returned about an hour later. "I set a trapline this morning out by the lake," he signed. "Should have beaver here soon."

Then he sat by the fire, and started working on the bundle of sticks he'd set to thaw the night before. She started a meal on the fire, using wild onions he'd hung up over the windows, and some more of the elk. When the food was ready, they ate by the fire, and when they were done, he retrieved the newly thawed branches and continued his work.

He measured them first and cut them evenly. Then he began to shape the longest ones into an oval frame. After which, he crossed weaved sticks into the frame, tying them in place with bits of rawhide cord.

She liked watching him work. Watching the intense focus as he bent and shaped the branches to his will, the small muscles in his hands and forearm rippling as he carved holes and shaped the ends with his knife. And she noticed then, for the first time, just how big his rangy hands were.

It was noon by the time he finished. He stood up and motioned her away from where she now lounged by the fire. She had been dozing between bouts of watching him work. He signed for her to sit, and showed her what he had made. They were snowshoes. He knelt in front of her and helped lash them to her moccasined feet.

His touch was practical and gentle but her body turned giddy.

Eventually, he was done and when he looked up, she felt her face stuck dumbly in that of a smile. He gave her a peculiar look, one of confusion, and she felt as if he could read all that her mind held.

He helped her up. And finally coming to grips with herself, she signed, "Where do we go?"

"I can't tell you," he signed.

It was cold outside, and even though he had draped a great thick buffalo robe over her shoulder, her legs still trembled. Her calves, exposed as they were to the wind, pricked with goose bumps. The snow was deep. At least a foot deep in most places, and in others it had piled up in big cloudy drifts.

He led her out behind the cabin, and she wondered where they could possibly be going. The snowshoes worked well, letting them both glide across the top of the snow at normal pace. But her feet were soaked after only a few steps, and then grew numb.

He led her through a gap in the pines, boughs bent by white pillows of snow, and then up a steep incline that followed along the sheer face of the mountain.

As they worked up along the ledge that wound around the mountain, he pointed to the horses below. They pawed at the snow, and he signed proudly that he had found this place two summers ago. Then he signed something about it being the perfect place to let the horses loose. She watched him as he surveyed his handiwork, somewhat distracted by the set of his shoulders.

The trail they followed wrapped sideways around the rock face, and then widened to a little gap where the mountain split apart, creating a narrow canyon. It was a rocky place and full of snow topped boulders. At this point, the cold finally caught up to her, causing her feet to pulse with fire, so soaked and chilled that they burned. The ends of her fingers felt like icicles. She began to shiver and as she shivered, she began to get mad.

"Stop," she cried out, and then signed vigorously, "where are we going?"

He laughed at her. Not a malicious laugh, but a knowing laugh, that said she would think herself foolish if only she knew what he didn't. Then he put his fingers to her lips as if to shush her, and signed, "you will see."

And she did see, for two hundred feet later, where the little box canyon opened a bit wider, it was filled with steam, and several hot springs dotted the floor of the small box canyon. Blue green pools of water radiating warmth, crowned in gold and ivory from excess mineral deposits, the steam rising from them, melting the surrounding snow to reveal the smooth slate gray of the canyon's stony bottom.

He guided her down the little trail, and then past the first, and the second pool, until they stopped in front of the third one.

"Here," he signed, motioning from her to the pool. "You wanted to bathe."

Then, before she could respond, he walked some ways off to a great flat stone, where he sat down with his back to her. Giving her some semblance of privacy.

Apaniaki glanced down at the hot spring. She could feel its warmth, the steam mixing with the cold air, and leaving her damp and hot and chilled. Goosebumps crawled her whole body then, but not from the mixture in the air, but from the man seated on the rock. This was much better than the bucket of snow and the rag.

She shrugged out of the buffalo robe, and then out of her buckskin dress. Working quickly and glancing every so often at the man on the rock to make sure he wasn't looking... or perhaps, in the hopes that he would.

Then she bent, naked by the pool, and tested the water with a hand. It was warm, hot even, but not burning. She lowered her body into it, and took several gasps as the blood in her body found its way back to icy limbs.

She lost herself in it for several moments, and then glanced back to check that Le-Vi was still there. And he was, stationed no more than ten feet away from her, and though she couldn't see his eyes, she knew that even now he watched for danger.

She realized then, in that small moment, that she had been filled with nothing but relief since that moment at the camp of the Crows. This man who had made the hairs on her arms stand at end since she'd met him. This was a man she could be a sits-beside-me-wife too.

Slowly, she waded to the edge of the spring and pushed herself up onto the gray stones. Then walking softly, cat like on the balls of her feet, she laid a hand on his back. And he started a bit at her touch, a tender touch, that froze him in place and brought blood to boil, and when he turned around, he looked at her with hungry eyes, the way he had seeing her at the lake.

THE EARLY MORNING LIGHT PEEKED through the windows of the cabin. Bright Eyes lay with her head on his chest. They had lain together all night, until they'd both finally collapsed from exhaustion. Him being the first to desist.

He shifted upwards and examined the lithe body that lay next to him, tiger striped by the sun and the window it was filtering through. He knew he was done for then. Done for in the worst sort of way. For she was his now, and he'd never known a feeling quite like it. He would kill for her. Die for her. Raze entire villages if a hair on her head was so much as touched.

She looked up at him, long lashed eyes flickering open just for a second, as if she was checking that he was still there, then she smiled a small, satisfied smile—a contented smile, before repositioning her head on his chest.

Levi stared blankly at the rest of the cabin, at the sunlight pouring in through dirty glass, and the small table in the center of the room. It wasn't a whole lot. But it felt like a hell of a lot more now than it had two days ago.

And he felt fear. The first real sort of fear that he'd felt for a long time. He had something to lose. It was a different kind of fear than he'd felt out on the trail, upon catching the sound of a twig snap or spotting Indian sign where he hadn't expected any. Different than the palms full of sweat just before a fight, or when his leg shook uncontrollably after a grizzly made a false charge. No, this was the sort of fear that could steal a man blind if he let it. Steal all his power and make the very thing he was afraid of—inevitable. It was the fear of loss, and loss was that long tortured, waking death.

He'd seen it work on his father, after his mother passed. Her death had made him a husk of a man. Every day after had been a slovenly attempt at suicide, casting himself off the cliff edge of a jug just to land in its baked-clay belly—a bit more broken, but no less alive. That was what grief did to a man. Loss turning him all inside out until there was nothing left to give. Made him go looking for fullness in all the places where it would never be. Turned him against his own son, even. He'd never hated him, Levi knew that much, no, he'd hated the universe, and Levi had simply been there to remind him of it. He never raised so much as his voice when he was sober.

But Levi had taken the lesson to heart, and the wild places had welcomed him. He was rootless. A wanderer. Nothing to attach to, and nothing to lose, at least until now. But even that had scared him, back in the cave with the arrow sticking out of his shoulder. The only thing he loved, which was the tall blue mountains, were just about the last thing anybody would ever be able to misplace. He liked it that way. He'd thought he'd figured it all the way out. If a man had to love, then it might as well be the biggest, heaviest most rock-solid thing on earth.

The girl shifted next to him, breaking out into a long stretch, the way a cat wakes up from an afternoon nap. He felt her skin press up against his, and it was enough to make him ready for another go at it. Then she sat up. The rays of sunlight cast her shoulders in gold, and her hair fell in messy strings across her face, lips formed a small, tired pout—what she could possibly be pouting about within seconds of waking he knew not. But that look made him want to do anything.

"Good morning," she said. She didn't sign it. She said it. Her Blackfoot tongue handling the English words awkwardly. She was picking up his words quickly, learning English far faster than he was learning Blackfoot for she seemed to have a head start on account of her father. Mor than that, her memory was excellent, for she'd explained to him some of how Blackfoot medicine worked, and how she had memorized the history of her people, and how every cure came with a song, and how all the animals had a story, and it seemed to him that only an agile mind would be capable of such a task.

"Good Morning," Levi said softly.

CHAPTER 17
BLACK CROW'S DREAM

Black Crow walked through summer fields. Ahead of him, his daughter played in the sweetgrass. Sun Boy rose in the east, and his rays danced across the field. Apaniaki was still small, still a little girl. His little girl.

Clouds towered in the North, great ivory pillars which seemed to hold aloft the rest of the far, big sky. They seemed to grow larger and closer each time he looked back at them.

Apaniaki picked up a grasshopper. She giggled as it skittered across her rotating hand.

Then thunder cracked the firmament, and Sun Boy was gone. Cold Maker had overtaken him.

Apaniaki cried out then and ran to him. The grasshopper had died. It lay still in the palm of her hand, a victim of the season.

"It was his time," Black Crow said. "Cold Maker has come."

"But, I liked him," Apaniaki said.

Black Crow looked around, and spotting a little snake, snatched it up. It was slow from the cold, and wrapped itself around his hand, coiling and uncoiling.

"Here is snake," Black Crow said. "He will be a good friend to you."

"But I don't want snake," Apaniaki cried, but she took the snake from him anyway. Then Snake bit Apaniaki, and she cried out again, for she was bleeding. She shook snake free from her hand, but then snake chased her, and bit her again. At this Black Crow despaired, and he tried to catch snake, to stop him from biting her, but then snake turned on him, and bit him on the hand.

Black Crow watched helplessly, for Snake's bite had immobilized him. He tried to pray to the Great One that he send something to protect his little girl from snake, but he could not, for he was paralyzed. The great one could not hear his thoughts, and he could not do the sacred dance to ask for the Great Ones help.

BLACK CROW WOKE GASPING. THE SOUND OF rain pattered gently on the outside of his lodge, and he immediately felt a deep chill. He felt Fox Kitten Woman move next to him. She was warm.

Black Crow cast the buffalo blanket off of him and sat straight up, trying to catch his breath, and clear his head.

"What is wrong?" Fox Kitten Woman asked.

"I have had a dream," Black Crow said. "But I know not what it means."

Fox Kitten Woman reached a hand up and slowly scratched his back as she had done many times before.

"They have been gone almost half a moon, and still Large Teeth and Gray Wolf have not returned," Black Crow continued.

"Is that what your dream was about?" Fox Kitten Woman asked.

"I need to see Red Beaver," Black Crow said.

He pulled on his buckskin pants, wrapped a buffalo robe about himself, and kissed Fox Kitten Woman goodbye. Outside, it was still raining, and Cold Maker had turned the soil outside his lodge to mud. Black Crow started off through the mud and rain to Red Beaver's lodge. The dream had deeply disturbed him, and he worried about Apaniaki. He should have gone with Large Teeth. If he had gone, he would have been able to protect her.

But he had not, fearing that he would slow them down, for he was an older man now, and unable to keep pace. Oh how he loathed getting old. For their was a time when he could ride for days straight without stopping to sleep, and could live off nothing more than a handful of dried meat and the fire in his belly.

He pulled the flap back to Red Beaver's lodge and slipped inside. The old man's fire was still burning brightly, and in front of it, sat his wise old friend, cross-legged and bright-eyed.

"Do you not sleep, wise one?" Black Crow asked. He only called his old friend Wise One when they were alone, and as a gentle rib.

Red Beaver smiled. "When one is visited so often in dream, sleep begins to feel like waking. Besides, I grow old. I need less of it now; I prefer to stare at the fire. The fire tells me things."

"I worry for Apaniaki."

"Sit my friend." Red Beaver motioned for Black Crow to sit down next to him. The old man leaned backwards, and retrieved his pipe, and then packed the bowl with tobacco taken from the pouch on his belt. Lighting the pipe with a stick from the fire, he took two long puffs, and gave it life. Then Red Beaver passed the pipe to Black Crow.

"Now, tell me this dream," Red Beaver commanded.

Black Crow recounted to him all that had occurred in his dream, and the old medicine man listened intently. When Black Crow had finished, Red Beaver asked him, "and the great one did not answer your prayers?"

"I could not pray," Black Crow said. "And then I woke up."

"You can pray now," Red Beaver said.

"Is it not too late?" Black Crow asked. "Has not what come to pass already happened."

"The great one moves freely between the seasons," Red Beaver said. "What has happened and what will happen are the same to him. Go and perform the sacred dance and pray for protection over Apaniaki. Tell me then what dreams you have."

Black Crow departed and returned to his lodge.

It was three days later, when Black Crow rose early in the morning and stood outside his lodge. He had performed the sacred dance, and he had prayed for protection over Apaniaki, but no further vision had come. Sun Boy rose in the east and chased Cold Maker away. The winds were warm, and it seemed that Cold Maker, at least for the coming day, had lost his battle with Sun Boy.

Black Crow saw movement then, along the horizon. Figures moving in the early morning light, made shadow and silhouette by Sun Boy's early rays. As the figures neared, Black Crow went to meet them.

It was the raiding party gone after Apaniaki. They

looked worn and haggard. Large Teeth was in the lead, and beside him stood Gray Wolf. They were on foot, and their clothes were dirty and muddy, as if they had walked many miles.

"What has happened?" Black Crow asked.

"A great evil befell us," Large Teeth said. "Napikwan stole our horses. He is a ghost. An evil spirit."

"Where is Apaniaki?" Black Crow asked.

"Napikwan has taken her," Gray Wolf replied. "I had gone ahead to see where the Kicked in the Bellies camped, and while I lay watching, I saw the one who rides with Napi. He brought the horses that he stole from our men and he traded them for Apaniaki."

"Did you not follow them?" Black Crow said.

"I went back to get the others," Gray Wolf said. "But when we went to go after them, snow had already covered their tracks."

"We were without horses," Large Teeth said. "We could not follow."

Black Crow grunted his dismay, but said nothing, for he was mad. Terribly mad, and he did not want to say a thing that he could not take back. Instead, he turned his back on them—the fools and cowards.

He returned to his lodge then, cut his braids, and scattered ashes over himself. After a time of this, he departed the camp, and climbed the mountain that he may find yet another vision and ask the Great One why he had ignored his prayers.

On the mountain, after a long time of fasting, Black Crow fell asleep. Apaniaki came to him then, but she was not a little girl any longer, as she had been in his first dream, for she was now a woman, and walking beside her was Napi the coyote.

She asked him, "Why do you cry for me, Father?"

"I have prayed to the Great One that he might protect you, and still Napi has stolen you," Black Crow said.

"Don't you see father?" Apaniaki replied.

"See what?" Black Crow replied.

"I am here, before you," his daughter said. "Am I not whole?"

When morning came, he woke, shivering, next to a great crackling fire. Red Beaver was next to the fire and looked pleased to see him.

"Cold Maker would have taken you if I had not come and built this fire," Red Beaver said.

Black Crow pushed himself up on an elbow. "I saw her in a dream. Beside her was Napi."

Red Beaver smiled at that and said, "I know."

"Did she come to you as well?" Black Crow asked.

"She did not need to," Red Beaver replied. "I saw how she looked at him when I mended his shoulder. She did not even know how she felt then, but I knew."

"Why didn't you tell me?" Black Crow asked. He shifted up to a sitting position and pulled the buffalo robe tighter around him.

"Would you have believed me?" Red Beaver asked.

"Maybe," Black Crow said.

"She is strong," Red Beaver said, "We cannot control what happens, only align our wills."

"Is she safe?" Black Crow asked.

"I think so," Red Beaver said.

LARGE TEETH PACED NERVOUSLY OUTSIDE OF Black Crow's lodge. It had been a week since they'd returned from their long walk. The journey had been grueling on foot, and he was still tired from it. Cold Maker had brought the snow, turning the ground to white. The snow crunched under foot now, for it had melted and refrozen since it last fell.

The others had not given him a hard time for failing to rescue Apaniaki, which was counter to what he had expected. Perhaps, because so many of the others had been with him. Or perhaps, because of the great evil they'd encountered, the Elk spirit that had returned to curse them. Many of the others still believed that it was a curse. Only he knew it to be a trick. A trick played by the Napikwan.

The flap of the lodge opened, and Black Crow poked his head out. He motioned for Large Teeth to enter.

Inside, Black Crow motioned for him to sit. Fox Kitten Woman fetched his pipe and handed it to him. Their fire was going nicely and kept the lodge very warm. Almost too warm, Large Teeth thought, as he felt himself begin to sweat.

When they had both smoked, Black Crow asked him why he'd come.

"I came to ask that you let me raise another war party," said Large Teeth.

"It is winter," Black Crow said. "Already Cold Maker chokes the mountain passes. I cannot risk more men on what is sure to fail."

"I have to look," Large Teeth said. "Apaniaki is your daughter, don't you want me to find her?"

Black Crow scowled. "And what is Apaniaki to you? Why do you care so?"

Large Teeth stammered then, somewhat taken

aback. Both by the suggestion, and Black Crow's apparent lack of concern.

"I want her be my wife," Large Teeth said.

"Ahh," Black Crow responded. "Have I not previously said no?"

"I will prove myself to you," Large Teeth said.

"You are not right for her," Black Crow said. "The answer remains no."

"I will still go—"

"—Do not say empty things." Black Crow said, raising an open hand. "You must go all the way if you speak it. So do not speak it unless you are prepared to do it, otherwise there will be no power in your words."

Large Teeth sat silently then.

Then Black Crow continued saying, "She has come to me in a dream. She tells me that she is safe, and that is all I can want as a father."

"I will raid the Parted Hairs then?" Large Teeth said. "Will this you allow?"

"This I will," Black Crow said. "On the plains Cold Maker is an ally."

CHAPTER 18
THE HORSE RAID

LARGE TEETH LOUNGED BY THE FIRE OF Steals Many Horses. His lodge was warm, and his wife, Buffalo Calf sat preparing them a meal. They had returned from hunting Buffalo earlier that day, having found a small group sheltering from the wind at the bottom of a coulee. While Cold Maker had not brought any snows for many sleeps, the ground was still white with it, and the winds still blew cold. Winter was not a bad time to hunt buffalo and was in fact the best time to harvest hides as they were at their thickest and warmest.

The camp that the band had picked for winter had already proven to be one of the best in recent memory. Herds looking for grass and water moved through the small pass to the North of them. The trees that lay at its bottom allowed enough cover for the men to hunt. In some places, because of the lay of the land, the snow was deceptively deep and when the buffalo spooked, they ran through these places and became trapped in the snow drifts making it easy for a hunter on foot to kill them. Such was the place where Large Teeth and Steals Many Horses had killed the Black Horns earlier.

Buffalo Calf Woman turned the small intestine of the animal inside out, so that the fatty part would be on the inside. She then packed the long skin tube with a thin strip of meat and spooned still warm blood taken from the beast. This, she boiled over the fire, and in doing so made a favorite meal of Steals Many Horses.

Large Teeth passed the pipe back to his friend. He watched him take a deep inhale and wondered if now was the time to ask him about raiding. Steals Many Horses was a good warrior, and a skilled horseman. He would be an asset on a winter raid. But he was also doing quite well, and after the failed rescue of Apaniaki and the long walk back, many had seemed quite pleased to spend winter close to camp.

But the failed rescue hung heavy on Large Teeth. He had lost much honor in the failure, even if the others in the band no longer spoke of it. The women giggled and whispered as he passed, and not in the way that they did when talking about his bed. And once he'd stood outside the tent of Yellow Dog and listened as the man had sung mocking words about his dishonor. The measure of a man were two things, his war honors, and the quality of his horses. Presently, Large Teeth was failing on both accounts. Increasingly, he worried, if he did not change his luck, he would soon be known for it, and his very presence would be a totem of evil. Should that happen, he would no longer be invited to raid, nor chosen for hunts. He would be relegated to camp fool, left wifeless, stationless, and no good to anyone much less himself.

But most worrisome was Black Crow's apparent lack of concern for Apaniaki. His vision had shown him that all was well with her, and so he had seemed content with that answer. It was bad luck to question the dreams of another, especially the dreams of a Chief, but still, Large Teeth could not help but wonder if this dream had come too easily. Sometimes one dreamed the dream they wanted to dream, because the alternative was too unbearable. He would never say these things aloud of course, and he felt guilty thinking them.

He thought then of his own dream, and the words of the Snake Woman. Perhaps after he raided the Parted Hairs he would make his horned bow. She had come to him since, showing him the horns of a Ram and telling him to speak to Blue Dog.

Blue Dog had told him of a place high up in the mountains, just on the edge of Crow country, where hot springs were. Blue Dog had made several bows of horn over the years, and thus he had explained his method. One must kill a ram, and taking the horns, set them to soak in a hot spring for three days, until they became pliable. Once the horns could be bent and unfurled they needed to be unwound and lashed flat and tight to a board to dry. They would dry straight enough, finally allowing a man to shape them much the same way he would a bow of Yew. But a horn bow would be a great weapon, firing faster and harder than any made of wood. Some had even been strong enough to pierce the great buffalo hide shields.

But despite all this, he had never really believed in the ways of his people, at least not fully. Perhaps, his own penchant for deceit had made him wary of others he did not know. He had often watched Red Beaver, and wondered at the truth of his warnings, or the convenience of his admonishments. Where the spirits will began and Red Beaver's will ended was not clear to him.

"I want to go raiding," Large Teeth said at last, breaking the silence. "Now is a good time. It has not snowed for many sleeps. The going there will be easy. We can ask Red Beaver to make an entreaty to Cold Maker so that he will release the snows after our raid and cover our tracks."

Steals Many Horses exhaled a long stream of smoke as Large Teeth spoke, and then played with the red ribbon that held his scalp lock in place. Finally, he said, "I have no need of more horses, and even less need for such a long journey."

"But the taking will be easy, for the plains people will not expect us to come in winter," Large Teeth argued. "We can have many horses for spring, take even more Buffalo during the Summer season."

"It is not necessary," Steals Many Horses said. "I have all I need here. You are too much in a hurry be wealthy, to be powerful. Those things come in time."

"I do not have time," Large Teeth said, his tone grave. "Already the others whisper that I have bad medicine… that I am bad medicine."

"They will forget and your time will come," Steals Many Horses said, waving a hand at the sky. "You are clever and a good warrior. Already you have a Buffalo Runner of your own. You cannot ride more than one at a time you know. Wait my friend, and this summer we will go on many raids, many hunts. Give them time to forget."

Large Teeth sat back and sulked, for he saw that there would be no moving Steals Many Horses from this position. Soon after, the food was ready to eat, and they cut off pieces of the sausage and ate their fill. It was good, and for a few brief moments, Large Teeth felt satisfied. It did not last though, for after a while it was time for him to leave and go back to his empty lodge, while Steals Many Horses would no doubt wear out Buffalo Calf Woman late into the night. Already he had seen him appraising her, and her him.

His thoughts turned to Apaniaki then and remembered the way she looked. How her hips moved when she walked and had not known he was watching. The tumbling of her hair in the sun. The heave and fall of her heavy bosom. What he would give to take her.

He got up suddenly then. Bid them goodbye and excused himself for the night. As he trudged back to his own lodge, he thought on the way forward.

He had already asked Gray Wolf and He Who Shouts Loudly about the raid, but they had responded much like Steals Many Horses. They had no desire to walk so long a way in the cold. It was then that he passed by the lodge of the young Throws Far, the leader of the Mosquito Society, the most junior of the warrior societies. Throws Far had never been on a raid, but he was clever and trustworthy. Perhaps, Large Teeth could raise a band from the younger, less experienced braves. It would be dangerous taking a group of green warriors on a winter raid however, and he wondered if Red Beaver and Black Crow would even approve.

But maybe this was a thing he could do without approval. After a successful raid, it would be hard to punish him for a thing. Or perhaps he could ask for approval and leave out who he took with him.

Large Teeth thought on these things as he entered his own empty lodge. He had moved out of his father's house the week before the raid and had expected Apaniaki to share it with him. But now he was alone. It was not a good thing for a man to live alone, with no woman to keep his fire, to cook his meals, or warm his bed. He stirred the warm coals and piled a bit of wood onto the fire. The lodge was dim, lit with only the warm amber light of the flame. He sat back, and shivered in his buffalo robe, waiting for the fire to grow. It was a lonely thing.

As he stared into the fire, he saw the face of Spotted Locust, but only for a second, then he blinked him away. Then he felt badly, for he remembered that day on the range. He remembered squinting against the dust raised by the buffalo. The bodies of Spotted Locust and his horse lying there. The mangled body of his friend, the white bones in his legs broken and exposed. He felt the rock in his hand. The coarseness of it. And heard the pop of Spotted Locust's head as he had bashed it in, the sound like a ripe melon cracking.

Large Teeth groaned and clutched his own head. He wanted to forget. To forget all of it. He forced it out of his mind, but it would not go. And then at last, he slumped backwards, paralyzed by the images of that day.

"WHO GOES WITH YOU?" RED BEAVER ASKED.

"I have not decided yet," Large Teeth said. "I have Throws Far and Red Owl for sure, but likely Steals Many Horses and some more good warriors."

Red Beaver gave him a suspicious eye, then said, "Throws Far and Red Owl are young."

"They will not be alone," Large Teeth said. He lied. But it was not really a lie, for he would ask Steals Many Horses to go once more. "But it will be good for them, and a winter raid will bring much honor and many horses."

"I will throw the bones," Red Beaver said, "If the

bones say it is ok, then you can have my blessing for the raid."

"And can you make an entreaty to Cold Maker that he may hold the snows until we strike?"

After a long thoughtful pause, Red Beaver said, "Come back tomorrow and you will have your answer."

When Large Teeth returned the next morning, Red Beaver was sitting outside his lodge. His shoulders were hunched against the cold, a coat of wolf furs drawn tight around them, and the lines on his face made more prominent by his scowl.

"It is mixed," Red Beaver said. "Coldmaker says that he will not help, but the bones say the raid is good."

"What did you see?" Large Teeth asked, doing his best to manage his bearing. He could not let Red Beaver see his desperation.

"Cold Maker told me that you should not come. That he is already holding the snow, but not for you. He says there is a great evil that stalks the land in the form of the Long Knives."

"I am not afraid of Long Knives," Large Teeth said. "They do not know the ways of the wild places. They make fires out in the open, and they smell from many miles away."

"This is Cold Maker's word," Red Beaver said.

"Then is that a no?" Large Teeth asked.

"I cannot tell you no, for the bones have said yes," Red Beaver said. "But I don't think you should go."

Large Teeth straightened then, relief washing over him.

"You must avoid the Long Knives," Red Beaver reminded him. "You must leave them alone, for Cold Maker fears them."

Large Teeth gave a quick huff and then left, saying

nothing. He was tired. Tired of riddles and dreams, and the old man and his schemes.

THE SIX OF THEM LEFT AT DAWN THE following day. Large Teeth in the lead, and behind him trailed Throws Far and Red Owl, and behind them walked Fox Boy, Heavy Runner, and Small Eyes. Hoarfrost crunched beneath their feet, and the cold bit their ears. It was 16 sleeps in the direction of Sun Boy's rising. There they would find the people that called themselves Lakota, or as the Piikani knew them, the Parted Hairs.

They were all young, so young in fact that Large Teeth was the only one that had even been on a raid. But they'd begun the journey into manhood across the last two summers. They had grown sturdy and strong. They talked in deep voices now, smiling and joking confidently. Large Teeth could tell that already they believed themselves to be great warriors, without ever even stealing a single horse. He balked at the idea, quite suddenly, even as his feet propelled him forward. He could not play nurse maid on a winter raid. It was typical to have one or two green braves on a hunt, or a raid even, if they had proven themselves trustworthy. After all, everyone had a first time. But it was always a raid with many summers of experience on it. This though, this was surely madness. And more than that, if Large Teeth did not come back successful, there would be hell to pay, for he had taken children, a fact everyone would no doubt realize.

The sky was blue and clear, and no clouds hung in it. Large Teeth thought about Red Beaver's dream then. Cold Maker feared the Long Knives and so held back his snows. But that had begun to worry him too, for how would they escape with Buffalo Runners if Cold Maker was not there to cover their tracks? It mattered not, the bones had said yes to the raid. Did that not mean all would be well?

Although both journeys had been on foot, this one filled Large Teeth with pride and strength. The walk back from the Crows was the worst of Large Teeth's life. Fifteen long sleeps full of shame and cold. They had left on horseback and returned on foot. He had brought dishonor to all Piikani. But this one was different, this one they had left on foot and would return with many horses, of this he was sure of. Raids solely for horses often began on foot, making the journey in to enemy territory safer with less chance of being seen. And the ride back, meant that they could steal many more horses, not having to care for an already exhausted remuda.

They moved quickly through the terrain, running in places, and walking in others. They stopped about three times a day to smoke and eat bits of pemmican from the pouches on their belts. At night they built a small fire to protect them from the cold, always seeking a low place in the land where the light of their fire would not be seen. The low places protected them from the cold north winds, and the hills they camped between rose as dark monoliths on either side of them.

They journeyed onward, moving quickly through the country. The prairie had turned into a land of death. A frozen waste of dead grass and hard ground, and a great yawning silence that only the sound of their footsteps disrupted.

After the tenth sleep they crossed over into the land of the enemy. There were no more fires to keep warm at night, for a fire can be seen for a long ways on the prairie. Instead the band lay next to each other for heat, sharing blankets, and shivering through the night. Already the others complained of the cold and talked regretfully about coming along.

Large Teeth counted it a miracle that no snows had fallen since they left. This was perhaps the most dangerous portion of their journey, for they were on foot, and ten sleeps away from their people in the dead of winter. If Cold Maker came before they secured the horses, they would have a hard time of it. For he still did not trust Red Beaver nor his dream about Cold Maker.

When they passed by the place where the Elk River left the Big River, they watched a party of Long Knives while hidden in heavy brush on a high ridgeline. They were a small party and seemed to be hunkered down for the winter. A keelboat floated lazily in the Big River, tethered to the bank by ropes and stakes.

Large Teeth and his band watched them from a little way off, all the while making sure that they remained hidden. The Long Knives built their fires big, and their lodges seemed rudimentary and inefficient, having an open face in places. In front of their camp, they had built a rampart from trees chopped down at the edge of the river, and dirt which they had piled high into an embankment. This would give them protection from an attack that came from the prairie, while leaving their backside protected by the river.

They looked weak to Large Teeth, and he did not understand why Cold Maker would be so afraid of them. All told, there were no more than ten of them, covered in furs and carrying guns. They moved around lethargically, almost lazily, oblivious to Large Teeth and his boys. There seemed to be something wrong with them, but Large Teeth could not quite figure out what it was.

They had brought with them no horses to steal, but behind their camp, hidden under gray tarps was wooden crating. This would surely hold trade goods and the medicine water which Large Teeth had heard so much about. Perhaps, even guns and powder.

He heard then the warning of Red Beaver, and so he waved his party off. They slunk back down the bluff which overlooked the party of Long Knives and continued in the direction of the Parted Hairs.

IT TOOK THEM SIX MORE SLEEPS TO FIND THE Parted Hairs. They had made camp at the bottom of two hills, mostly hidden from sight, and in an easily defensible place. The Parted Hairs had left no guards on the hills, as they surely would have if it had been summer, for they were obviously not expecting a raid so deep into winter.

Large Teeth laid on his belly, watching the goings on below, and smiled proudly at the little camp. The Parted Hairs had many horses. Most of them held a way off so that they could graze, and only tended to by a couple of young bucks who returned to the camp to warm themselves by the fire. Their prized Buffalo Runners were held in the middle of the camp where they could not be easily stolen.

Throws Far lay on his belly next to him, his bow in hand.

"We have made it," Throws Far said. "I will take my first scalp tonight."

"No," Large Teeth said. "We come to steal not to make war. We kill no one if we can avoid it."

Throws Far scowled at this and did not respond.

Large Teeth had been worried about this. Worried about taking braves so young with him. They did not understand what could go wrong.

He glanced at Sun Boy, high in the sky, and whispered that they must withdraw until night time. They took shelter in a small arroyo two miles away from the camp. It was a rocky and barren place, good for nothing but hiding coyotes where no one would find them. The others lounged, occasionally pacing in order to keep their body temperature up. It was not overly cold, and although they had become accustomed to it, sitting still for long periods of time allowed an unbearable chill to invade the body.

As he sat there, he worried about them. They thought only of counting coup and having a lodge pole filled with many scalps. Large Teeth had been much the same a year ago, maybe he still was. Why else would he be here in the dead of winter, with young braves woefully unprepared for what lay in front of them? His thoughts turned then to Apaniaki. The girl with moonlit eyes and spider black hair. It was shameful to become so obsessed with a woman. He knew this, but still, he could not avoid it. Could not stop it. She was beautiful of course, but there was more to it than that. With her at his side, he would be respected by all the bands. Black Crow was powerful and had no sons. To be his son-in-law would bring great opportunity, if he could but gather war honors to himself.

Steals Many Horses had been right when he had said the People were all that mattered. But he had been wrong about wealth. Wealth was sons and horses and war honors. Black Crow's line would die with him. Even Apaniaki was not his blood child. Having sons was a hard thing. Much could go wrong during the nine moons, and much often did.

Large Teeth remembered then the stories of the old days, many seasons before his time, when the People had not had a single child born to them in a full season. Then the next year they only had three born to them, but all came out sickly. None had survived the winter. The band had decided to raid after that, but instead of horses they had stolen women. They stole the daughters of the Crows, and the Parted Hairs, and even the Root Eaters who lived where Sun Boy rested. The People had grown strong after that, but this had made them many enemies.

Securing more Buffalo Runners on this raid would put him in a good position to hunt this summer and to retrieve Apaniaki. It was not lost on him, that should this raid be successful, he would earn the undying loyalty of the ones he had brought with him. For all of them, this would be their first true raid. While it was true that Throws Far and Red Owl had already counted their first coup, for the others, this was their first chance to become men. That was not a debt easily forgotten.

In the distance, he watched Cold Maker gather his clouds. Was it possible that he planned to help them despite the Long Knives. The clouds gathered throughout the afternoon, and filled Large Teeth with hope that they would have an ally on their escape. The words of Red Beaver still nagged him, but not because Cold Maker seemingly refused to help them, but *why* he refused to help them. How could Cold Maker, one so powerful, fear the Long Knives. This seemed unthinkable. Cold Maker was a powerful force. He did not cower beneath the wishes of man. For a long time, the Blackfeet had treated him with respect, and now he withheld his snows for fear of the Long Knives. What did this make of the Piikani?

Were they not foolish then to treat Cold Maker with so much reverence?

Red Beaver was weak, Large Teeth thought. Cold Maker could fear no one. Red Beaver had lied, but his own weakness was in the lie, put upon Cold Maker who could not be weak. Always looking to nature and talking of dreams. Always, "we can't do this for Cold Maker, or Bear, or Raven says it is too dangerous, or it is unwise." It may be best if the Blackfeet knew no gods, he thought, for than they would be truly free. They would be free to make their own way, by their own strength, without the meddling of old men.

Nonetheless, Large Teeth watched in hope as Cold Maker mustered his might in the North. He watched as the long billowing towers of Cold Maker's wrath formed.

WHEN NIGHT FELL, THEY WORKED THEIR WAY back to the camp of the Parted Hairs. They sat silently at the top of the hill surveying the camp. When the two guards that watched over the grazing herd, returned to their lodges and their fires to warm themselves, Large Teeth sent Throws Far with the others to steal the herd.

He watched them run off, and when he could no longer see them, he, himself, slunk downwards toward the camp.

He picked his way through the lodges, careful of his sound. And then finally, finding the herd of Buffalo Runners, he gave a sharp sigh of relief.

Then Large Teeth was atop the nearest horse. It was a stout gray stallion. Behind him trailed two other Buffalo Runners that he towed along with rawhide cordage. He heard shouts behind him and kicked the horse to a steady trot. The warm wind was still on his face and the camp of the Parted Hairs lay behind him. It was dark out, and he squinted against the steady blackness. Cold Maker had covered the moon, and as all of the previous snows were melted, there was nothing but blackness. He would have to trust the horse to keep its footing.

He passed over the bluff, and caught the sound of steady hooves somewhere in the distance. Throws Far and the others had made off with the rest of the herd. He listened as more shouting came from behind him. The Parted Hairs had caught sight of him as he was leaving their camp and were now raising the alarm.

He wondered if they would try to follow, but he had no intention of sticking around long enough to tempt them. He kicked the gray stallion in its ribs and brought him to a gallop.

He ran him for about a mile and then let him settle into a steady lope. The most important part was now putting distance between them and the camp of the Parted Hairs. This was not always easy, for if one pushed a horse too hard, he would easily become tired and slow, but conversely, if he moved him too slowly, then it gave their pursuers time to catch up should they bank on pushing their own horses hard. Evasion was a dance, a delicate game of ceding ground and gaining time. It was six sleeps to the Big River, and ten more after, and the Parted Hairs would cross over the river even though it was Piikani lands.

It was the middle of the night by the time he caught up with the others. He heard the dull clop of hooves on the frozen prairie first, then a horse whinnied, and his own answered. Two more snorted. He heard then the telltale bird whistle of Throws Far that questioned whether he was friend or foe. Large Teeth responded with his own call.

He brought his horse up alongside Throws Far. "How many?" he asked.

"Twenty," Throws Far replied.

"Did you lose anyone?" Large Teeth asked.

"None," Throws Far replied. "They all did well. They were silent and brave, and Red Owl counted coup on one of the guards, and Heavy Runner took his first scalp."

Large Teeth stifled a flash of anger. He had told them not to kill. Killing would make it more likely they would be followed. "This is good," Large Teeth replied simply, deciding against chastisement, at least for the moment. To show disfavor now would do nothing but cause resentment. What was done was done.

"The Buffalo Runners?" Throws Far asked.

"Only these three," Large Teeth said. "The others were too far inside of their camp, and those had guards."

"We waited for you," Throws Far said. "When you did not come, we began to grow worried and thought maybe we should go back."

"It is good that you didn't," Large Teeth said. "All was well. But I was spotted leaving camp. They know that we have raided them."

A look of concern crossed Throws Far's face.

"This is fine, we must simply hope they do not follow. This is why I told you not to kill." Large Teeth could not help himself. The chastisement he'd planned to avoid came tumbling out of him. "Cold Maker may yet help us though. For this afternoon, I watched him in the North as he built his strength."

"We should keep going then," Throws Far said. "We have far to go before we get to the Big River."

THE RED ORB OF THE SUN BROKE THE horizon slowly. It was a bloody red, and an orange, and all was still, except they who moved across the plains. They had switched horses throughout the night to always keep a fresh mount beneath them. The temperature had dropped drastically in the latter part, and there was a fresh coating of frost on the dead grass and the dirt. Despite that, Cold Maker still withheld his snows. The air was dry and crisp, and even though the clouds piled high to the North, they seemed to hold steady.

This was not good. His men were tired. The journey had been long before this, and they had not bothered to stop and build a war lodge, for there was little game to hunt. In fact, they had seen no game close enough for the taking on the whole trip, and now the meat pouches at their belt were empty. On top of this, Large Teeth knew that the Parted Hairs would follow, for they had killed while in their camp, and without Cold Maker to stamp out their trail, the Parted Hairs would have no reason not to. Large Teeth only hoped they had made away with enough horses to limit the size of whatever party the Parted Hairs sent after them.

Hunger had turned his belly into a knot of wood, and the lack of food had begun to make him sore. He imagined that the others felt similarly. They could not survive this constant cold on empty bellies. An empty belly made the cold all but unbearable. Even he wanted to moan and whine, so surely they did as well. But they held their bearing like men, their spirits bolstered by the mass of horseflesh they now led.

It was midday when they passed a place where the land moved upward and gained territory from the sky, and he sent Throws Far up it, to see if they were followed. Throws Far returned in a hurry, saying that he saw riders maybe a day behind them.

Large Teeth scowled. This was not good. A day was nothing.

"How many did you see?" Large Teeth asked.

"I could not tell," Throws Far said. It was then that Large Teeth realized just how young the brave was. The shadow of worry, and naive concern on his face making him look every bit of his sixteen summers. They were all just children. Children trying to be men, and he had dragged them out here. Guilt flooded Large Teeth, and he again wondered if he had been wrong to talk them into the raid. He shook the thoughts off and hardened his face in the direction they traveled. They would make it, and they would no longer be children when they got there. They would return to camp as warriors. He would make sure of it.

"We must ride hard, and change mounts often," Large Teeth said. "And we slaughter a horse next time that we stop."

They broke into whoops at this news and spurred their horses into a run. The promise of a full belly giving new life. Large Teeth smiled at this. This story may yet be well told around the fires.

That night they picked out the smallest, weakest looking horse and killed it. They gorged themselves on its lean meat. The other braves were happy for it, and happy for the fire they'd built to cook it. They had ridden hard all afternoon and had undoubtedly gained ground on the Parted Hairs. Now was where the dance got dangerous. They could push on and wear themselves out on the chance that they outran them, or they could rest, and strengthen themselves on the chance that the Parted Hairs caught up to them anyways. Large Teeth did not fear a skirmish. They would fight if they had to.

His thoughts turned to Cold Maker then. He wished Cold Maker would release his snows. But the words of Red Beaver again rang in his ears, "Cold Maker fears the Long Knives and holds back his snows." But this time he heard opportunity in the words.

What if Cold Maker had nothing to fear. What if the Long Knives were no longer alive. The beginnings of a plan formed in Large Teeth's mind. The Long Knives had looked weak and unprepared when they had passed them. How hard would it be to kill them and free Cold Maker from his bindings in the North. Would he not thank them by hiding their tracks from the Parted Hairs.

Large Teeth took another bite of horse flesh and smiled at the fire. This was a plan. A good plan.

The next four sleeps passed slowly and were filled with dread. When he was not watching Cold Maker's might grow, and praying for him to come, he was busy twisting backwards in the saddle and searching for any sign of the Parted Hairs that trailed them. They rested for three hours every night, and then rode on. They switched horses often, keeping them fresh, but still pushing them as hard as they could go. The temperature dropped, and the cold became overly bitter, of a brutal kind he'd rarely known. But the skies directly overhead remained clear and blue, and dry.

In the early morning of the fourth day, when it was still dark, they approached the camp of the Long Knives. The Parted Hairs had somehow closed the gap between them the day before and were no more than half a day's ride behind. Large Teeth watched the flickering yellow cookfires of the Long Knives below.

"What do you think?" Throws Far asked.

"I will leave it to you all to decide," Large Teeth said. Then he told them of Red Beaver's dream, and the fear of Cold Maker, and of the warning to stay away from the Long Knives. Then he explained the logic to them. That killing the Long Knives would mean Cold Maker was once more free, and that he would help them with the Parted Hairs and hide their tracks.

When he had finished the others sat silently. Then it was Red Owl that spoke first. "We attack."

AS SUN BOY ROSE IN THE EAST, LARGE TEETH and his band stalked close to the camp of Long Knives. Stealing at night was one thing, but killing yet another, for it was said, that should a warrior be killed at night, his soul would wander, and he would not be able to find the Sandhills of their ancestors. So, if there was a real chance of death, they never attacked before Sun Boy had risen.

The Long Knives had stationed a single guard. One who had fallen asleep, bundled so warmly in his Buffalo coat. Large Teeth stole forward, his knife ready, bow over his back.

He missed his guns, the one the Napikwan had stolen back, and now carried the weapons he was most familiar with. He could shoot twenty arrows in the time it took to reload a Long Knife's gun. Red Owl trailed him as Throws Far led the rest of the band around to the other side of the camp. The Long Knives appeared to still be sleeping.

Large Teeth crept quietly over the rampart that

the Whites had built, moving cautiously so as to keep an object between him and the guard at all times. The muddy ground inside the camp had frozen hard, and he was deathly silent. When he was inside, he crept towards the guard from behind.

He plunged the knife deep into the neck of the sleeping man, and he gave no shout, only a shudder, his eyes flicking open in shock to find that the deed had already been done, his waking moments also his last. Large Teeth lifted his scalp quickly and expertly, taking a firm grip on the hair, and slicing a line across the top of the man's forehead. The trophy released steam as he peeled it back from the ivory skull, so suddenly had it been exposed to the frigid air.

The others stalked through the tents with knives and hatchets and dispatched the sleeping men just as quickly. A shot rang out. The braves gave sudden whoops, their hatchet work growing frantic and messy, as silence no longer mattered.

A man exited the tent nearest Large Teeth, and he tried to level his gun enough to fire, but Large Teeth covered the ground between them with three long strides and plunged his knife repeatedly into the man's breast. The gun went off uselessly into the air, setting Large Teeth's ears to ringing. Then the man lay dead at his feet, and he scanned his surroundings, before again lifting the scalp.

"It is over," Red Owl shouted triumphantly. "They are all dead."

Whoops went up from the others, and howls of victory, and as quickly as that, the fight was done. The Long Knives dispatched in less time than it took to eat a morning meal.

"Come quickly," Throws Far called. Large Teeth ran to him, and found a naked body, for Throws Far had begun to strip the corpse of its clothing. The body was covered in red sores. Throws Far stood back from it, in disgust, and some terror.

"The others are like that too," Red Owl said, coming up alongside him.

So this was why the Long Knives had been so weak. Why the fight had so moved so quickly.

"The evil scabs," Large Teeth said. By this time, the other braves had gathered. "We must leave now, before this evil follows. Take nothing from this place." Then Large Teeth tossed the two bloody scalps in his hand on the ground, and the others did as well, until they lay in a small bloody pile.

After that, they rode hard from the camp of the Long Knives and again crossed over the Big River. And it was late afternoon when Cold Maker released his snows.

It had worked, Large Teeth thought to himself. They had freed him, and now he helped hide them from the Parted Hairs. The snow fell in big wet flakes, slowly at first, but then the winds grew fast, and Cold Maker howled terribly, until the snow came in sideways and forced them to seek shelter in a grove of cedars. The men sheltered, happy that they had been saved, but scared that the evil of the Long Knives still followed.

"We must never speak of this to anyone," Large Teeth said, for he had grown ashamed of the thing that they had done.

"We must swear an oath," Red Owl said. "We must make a pact in blood."

Throws Far stepped forward, drawing his knife from the sheath at his hip, and he sliced a long red line down his palm. The others followed, and they clasped hands, so that no one may know that they had disobeyed the words of Red Beaver.

CHAPTER 19
THE WOLVES

HE BUILT THE SWEAT LODGE IT A LITTLE WAY off from the cabin but still in view. The base of it was made from logs chinked with mud. Making the mud was a slow, miserable process as everywhere the ground was frozen. So, he broke the ice at the edge of the lake and took mud from the bottom with a bucket and mixed it with frozen earth clawed up with his tomahawk to give it volume.

The top of the lodge, and the entrance, would be covered with buffalo blankets. And when it was finished, there would only be enough room for two people to sit inside, being as it was only about four feet tall.

While he worked on the lodge, Apaniaki kept herself busy around the cabin cleaning and curing the Beaver hides that he had laid up. Often when the sun started to sink lower in the sky, he would watch her exit the little cabin and then wander up the hill behind it. She did this several days in a row, and each time he wondered where she went and what she got up to, until at last he decided to follow.

He found her at the top of the hill, the slate gray

mountains towering behind her, and all-around stood quaking pines. She sat silently, not doing anything. Just sitting and looking, watching the world spin by below her. At Levi's approach, she looked up and a peaceful smile fluttered across her lips. He was about to speak, but she put a finger to her lips, and motioned for him to sit beside her.

Levi sat down and said nothing.

He looked out at the land below them as it fell away in great heaving sighs. Great pines, still green, sagged under the weight of snows gone by. Great Firs and Aspen fought for supremacy amongst the gaps, and everywhere lay white pillowed ledges where great walls of brush had gathered the snow.

White throated sparrows bickered further down the mountain before breaking cover and dancing across an ice blue sky. The sky was mirror smooth, above reflecting below. Great mounds of white clouds scattered across its face like so many piled drifts, and here and there, its jeweled surface caught the sun, spinning gold.

The sparrows left, chasing each other to further valleys, and all that was left was a great silence. A humming stillness that filled out the melody of their slow synchronous breathing.

Levi's breath crystallized as soon as it left his body. And he thought then that the cold was as a living thing, a force that overpowered and arrested all life, if only for a time. Death. A beautiful white death. A redeeming death.

"Why do you come up here," he asked.

"Do you not like it?" she asked.

"It's beautiful, sure." Levi responded.

She smiled at him, and said something in her own tongue that he did not quite understand. At his confusion, she tried to sign it and he wasn't quite sure that he got her meaning, but he thought that she was just saying, it was "to be" or "being."

He didn't press her further. He felt it—the pulse of nature, the gentle hum of the earth, a place in the order of it all. A rightness, that stood outside of a man and his experience.

THREE DAYS PASSED, AND LEVI HAVING fasted, added the buffalo hide covers to the top of the little dugout, securing them with rawhide cords attached with toggles. Outside the little sweat lodge, he built a great fire and set the round stones taken from the edge of the lake within.

Apaniaki signed for him to undress, and to sit inside the lodge. She then took the stones from the fire with a forked stick and piled them on the bed of gravel in the center of the lodge. Closing the flap behind her, she sat and dipped a pine bough in the bucket of water and then brushed it on the heated rocks.

She did this every so often, carefully managing the heat and steam in the lodge, and it was not long before he began to sweat. They sat in silence for a long time after that, and long after Levi had grown hot and uncomfortable, she finally signaled that the sweat was done. The sweat was to purify, she signed.

Outside, the cold air felt good on his skin, refreshing even, and he felt a lightness about him.

At the cabin, Apaniaki made him to lie down on the buffalo blanket set out in front of the fire. She signed for him to try to sleep. Then she bent over a bowl and ground a paste of herbs and roots taken from her medicine bag, which she boiled in the kettle over the fire. Levi recognized none of the plants.

Then she applied the paste to him, pausing every so often to chant and sing, occasionally making him take some of it on his tongue. Then taking an eagle bone whistle, she blew shrieking notes over his body.

He started to flush, and felt his head grow foggy and distant. He felt warm. Too warm, like he was burning up with a fever. But the whistling helped somehow. And then he was on top of a high mountain set so high that its crown was above the clouds.

Behind him he heard Apaniaki saying something to him, but when he turned, she was no longer there. Instead, there lay a coiled snake, and it transformed then to an old woman. The old woman drew close to him. Just then the clouds rose, climbing higher towards the top of the mountain, leaving him and the old woman shrouded in a thick fog that blocked out all of the sun.

"You have taken what was not given," the old woman said.

"She has chosen freely," Levi responded.

"But the choice was not hers," the old woman replied. "She was Black Crow's to give."

Then she slipped back into the fog and disappeared. And then darkness fell, and the mountain came alive with the sounds of the night.

Two wolves came to him then. They were old wolves from a different place, and of a kind that he had not seen before. And he asked them what the old woman had meant.

"These are not our lands," the wolves replied. "We cannot help you here."

"Then how am I to find my way from this darkness?" Levi asked.

"Ask our little brother, the Coyote, for this is his game."

"And where should I find Coyote?" Levi asked, but the wolves had already departed.

He woke after that and found that it was morning. Apaniaki lay next to him on the floor. She looked peaceful. He heard the wind blowing outside and eased himself out from beneath the buffalo blankets she'd laid over top of him. It was snowing outside. Again.

He stirred the fire in the hearth and piled more wood onto it. Then he sat thinking on the dream. It didn't seem like much of a dream.

Apaniaki woke, and shifted herself up onto an elbow. She motioned for him to come near.

"What of your dream?" she asked.

He told her the story then, signing as best he could and filling in the gaps with the little Blackfoot he had learned.

She nodded along, asking a question here or there, and then sat silently when he had finished. After a while she got up and started to make breakfast. Levi watched her work, and held his tongue, even though he wanted desperately to know what she thought it meant. She seemed deep in thought, and the palor had left her face white as a canvas.

Finally, she turned to him, and signed, "You must take me back. If we are to be happy you must ask my father's permission. It is the only way."

"The snake?" Levi asked.

"It is him," Apaniaki replied. "The old snake woman has given him her medicine. Snake medicine is strong medicine."

"And what of the wolves?" Levi asked.

"They are wolves from your lands. The helpers of your people..." Apaniaki signed, "from the far lands of the Long Knives. They have no power here. But coyote is little brother to all wolves, and he has favored you, and so you have a friend. But he is both trickster and creator, causing much trouble. Much heartbreak. He is change."

"We can't leave yet," Levi signed.

"When the snows melt, we can go. Maybe two moons," she responded.

"Yeah," Levi said.

APANIAKI LAID WIDE AWAKE THAT NIGHT, staring at the dimly lit rafters of the cabin. Levi lay next to her, the heat from his body a small, soothing comfort. He snored gently, and she rationalized that this was the reason she could not fall asleep, but even as she did so, she knew that was not true. It was her own heart that troubled her, and her head, which would not find quietness. She replayed Levi's words over, the ones wherein he had described his dream, and each time, they troubled her more deeply. His dream had made it clear. Their love was not ordained by her father, and thus, would only bring trouble.

The very thing that she had tried so hard to avoid, tried to guard against. She'd given her heart away to someone, to something that could not be. That it was his dream, and not hers, was even more troublesome. She would be his heartache, and the thought of that made her sick.

She loved him. Burned for him with every fiber of her being. He was gentle, and kind, at least to her, and the things he cared for, but to everything else, to foe or enemy, he was to be feared. He had made the wild places his home, and mastered them. Mastered both beast and man, and done so without a tribe. Even this place was a testament to him. He had carved a good place to live out of the cold hard mountains, and kept them well fed even in winter. She looked at the stack of Beaver pelts piled high in the far corner of the cabin. Enough furs to trade for anything they could want. And she wondered at that, at the fact that whatever he touched seemed to multiply.

And despite all of this, how could they fight against what was foretold? Their only chance was her father. The only way was her father. But would Levi go? He had no reason to. No reason to believe any of this. He was not Piikani.

CHAPTER 20
HOME SICK

WINTER PASSED MORE QUICKLY AFTER THAT. The days grew in length, but yet their passage seemed to quicken. Apaniaki did not mention the dream again, though it was always on her mind, for she was committed to not letting it touch them—their happiness or love—at least for the two moons. Her facility with English had grown, outpacing his ability to use her language, and often they no longer had any need to sign, talking to each other in a mix languages.

When the sun fell in the chilly evening, and Levi sat piddling over some bit of harness or fixing a steel trap, and she stood nursing the stew over the fire, she tried to soak the moment up. She devoted her mind to it, and her heart, for if life had given her one chance at happiness, she would surely remember it.

Often, they sat high up on the mountain surrounded by the great silence, and the birds sang sharply, and the pines whispered their sad songs, and she sat in the moment, feeling heavy, transcribing it to memory.

And when he held her down against the rough

hide of the buffalo covering and she felt the power of him between her legs, and his mouth searched for her own, desperate and hungry, she carved the moment into the very pillars of her being.

Yet, the moments were stained. Tainted with the terrible anxiety of an unknown future. And while things are often sweeter for the knowledge that they must end, the taste had become bitter, and she feared it would poison the whole.

And so the Big Winds Moon turned over in anticipation of the Budding Tree's moon, and she made love to him as if every time would be their last, and afterwards, dreamt of children's laughter and a lodge smelling of sweetgrass. It was always summer in her dreams. But in the early light of the morn, when she lay awake, staring at the cabin's roof above, Levi fast asleep next to her, she wept gently, ever so gently, so that she would not wake him.

"Why do you cry?" Levi asked once, after she'd woken him.

"The dream," she said after some time.

"We don't have to go back," Levi said. He pressed his face into her neck.

"We shall always cast one eye over our shoulder," Apaniaki said. "Always be aware for danger."

"We would anyways," Levi said.

"But it has been told," she said.

"Yeah," Levi rolled over onto his back. Away from her. And it felt in that moment as if he'd rolled a thousand miles away.

"I'm scared," Apaniaki said.

"I know," Levi said absently, turning back over to face her.

"No, you don't understand," she pushed herself up a little way in bed, then taking his hand in hers pressed it onto her belly.

"No," he said in unbelief, grinning large, and even in the dim light she could see his eyes spark with excitement.

"You're... how can you tell?"

"I know," she said. "It is still early, but I know."

"I'm going to have a son," he said, collapsing backwards.

⸙

It was early morning. Levi sat, smoothbore in a mittened hand, hidden behind a fallen log still glazed in ice and snow. Loki lay next to him, and a warm wind came down off the mountain. He'd seen a robin the day before and spotted some of the first green shoots of grass that signaled the coming of Spring. His eyes searched the trees for movement.

They had plenty of meat back at the cabin, and for the most part had eaten well all winter, which was in part due to the steady access to Beaver. If a deer passed down the game trail in front of him, he wasn't all that sure he would even shoot it. He was mostly here because he was sick of four walls, and because he did his best thinking in the quiet stillness. He had some superstitions about greeting the rising sun in person, and the peculiar idea that spending the early morning outside thickened one's blood.

The truth of the matter was that hunting gave him a reason to be there. He'd heard tales of city folks and such taking nature walks, and it never did make sense to him, but he supposed that is exactly what he was doing, just with extra steps, and the comfort of a gun.

Two moons had come and gone. Apaniaki had grown distant. Two moons was a long time to have something hanging over one's head, and although she tried to hide it, he could tell that his dream had changed things between them. It had lodged somewhere deep inside her and taken firm root. She'd tried not to let on that it had, but he knew, he could read every flicker of fear and flutter of heart that whipped across those shiny blue eyes. She worried for their child, his child.

After she had told him about the pregnancy, he had resisted the idea of returning to her people even more strongly. The danger of travel was far too great when she was with child. But she had brought it up to him again on the walk back from the mountain, back from their quiet time of sitting.

He had argued that he didn't see why it was necessary, that they were happy together, and he could take care of her. He saw only potential for disaster.

She had replied shakily, with a tremor in her voice, that she feared it was the only way, that if she did not do this thing now... She feared that both of them, and their child, would be living under a "dark star" and just waiting for it to fall.

He had not ceded the point then, but rather, the next morning, after a restless sleep and much thought, he woke telling her they would go. She had burst into tears at that, and thrown herself into his arms. They'd not spoken on the matter again, but set the date for the night of the Budding Tree's Moon.

And now that day had come.

Fate was a thing that hung heavy, and it hurt him to watch her labor beneath it. Levi had always been taught to pay no mind to fate, for what it did or did not do could change as often as God liked. All a man could do in the face of eternal uncertainty was face his doom head on, and go straight at it, whether it was win, lose, or draw. There was honor in that. And that's what he planned to do now.

But it was a harder thing to do when kin was the prize wrestled for.

He had no real desire to tangle with her people again, and he wondered how their war party had fared. He had left ten of them horseless, and killed another. Assuming they had walked back, which was likely, he could only imagine how much they hated his guts. And that was the rescue party her father had no doubt sent after her. Now he was supposed to just ride back and get her father's blessing, all because of a dream...

Fuckin hell, he hated it. Hated all of it and could barely trace the line of action that had gotten him to this place. He cursed the Old Man then, the one that had sent him on this wild goose chase. And he cursed the godforsaken boneyard he'd fallen into while trying to hide from the Utes. He had a pile of furs stacked up in the back of the cabin. Trapping had been good. He'd gotten away from the Utes, and who knows if the curse from that Indian graveyard had even been real. If the events were taken on their face, he didn't really seem all that free of it even now.

But the truth of it was, he hadn't believed in that curse since the morning he saw her. He'd gone after Apaniaki because he wanted her. He'd wanted her bad ever since that first time at the lake. She'd crawled up under his skin like a splinter and wouldn't leave, and now she was carrying his child. The truth was the curse was just a damn good reason to go chasin' a woman all across God's country.

Levi stood up then, and rolled his shoulder forward, stretching it against the chill. It felt good. It had finally healed up, no small part of that was thanks to Apaniaki. In the end, he supposed it all made sense.

He supposed that Large Teeth would search for them as soon as the winds blew warm and the earth turned green. Apaniaki was a lot of woman, and if he was in the brave's shoes, he couldn't rightly see letting all this go. Besides, this was a land for men. Securing their future might rest solely with making friends of her people. He couldn't see taking her back East or leaving her at a Fort. He couldn't put her through a life of derision, a life of being the Indian whore.

No, the mountains were his home now, and they would live in them, and her with him, come what may. They would go.

CHAPTER 21
AMBUSHED

LEVI BROUGHT THE HORSES UP FROM THE box canyon behind the mountain. They'd fared well, all things considered. A bit skinny, but not sick, nor weak. They had a hardness to them that only cold winds could bestow.

He tied the horses up outside the cabin, giving both a handful of mesquite beans he'd saved back. He liked the name Star Runner. It was a good name for a horse.

He loaded each down with a healthy supply of food, some pemmican, some mesquite beans, and a large quantity of jerked venison. They could hunt on the way, but they would not go hungry for he'd laid up plenty of meat over the winter.

He had just finished tying down the packs, when Apaniaki emerged from the cabin. She looked stunning in the morning sun's gentle light. She glowed with warm vitality; ochre skin lightened from the long winter, black hair, and piercing blue eyes. She was draped in a heavy buffalo coat, two sizes two big for such a slender frame, yet she wore it easily, with shoulders back.

He helped her onto the little black mare, and then mounted Star Runner. She smiled at him, and then looked back at the little cabin with sadness in her eyes.

"We'll be back," Levi said. "Don't you worry."

"I have... never been so happy," Apaniaki said slowly. She said it in English, slowly and fitfully. She was not yet completely fluent, but well on her way.

The weather was warm and much of the snow had begun to melt, turning the trace down into mud. They dismounted in places to walk the horses so they might not lose their footing. And as they worked their way off the mountain, the land fell away below them. Pine trees shimmering beneath easy spring rays, like a long and fertile green sea.

They saw herds of elk gathered to eat the new shoots of grass in the valley below. Above them a hawk circled, then two, riding warm winds higher and higher, in search of a meal. Once they saw a mama bear and her cubs, but they were a long way away and posed no threat. They sat the horses for a minute, watching the cubs tumble and play. Levi's heart swelled at the scene, at the image of new life. He glanced at Apaniaki, who was engrossed in the bears, giggling as the two cubs wrestled each other and threw up small paws in powerful displays of intimidation. Their momma stood by, guarding against danger.

They camped that night under a clear sky and the stars hung in bright multitudes. Levi built a hat full of fire beneath a great conifer, and Apaniaki lay as close as possible next to him. He alternated between staring into the fire, and staring at the stars. Together, they lulled him into a gentle sleep.

On the third day, they spotted a small band of Crow warriors working their way across the pass opposite them. Levi pulled up on the reins of Star Runner, and guided Apaniaki into the cover offered by a small grove of pines. The Crow were a long way off, but even at distance, Levi could make out the bright reds and yellows painted on their horses and the shiny war bonnets that crowned their heads. There were five of them. Probably young bucks on the warpath.

When the warriors had passed out of sight, they continued on. Levi needed no directions from Sun or Stars, for he knew the way down out of the mountains well, having travelled it many times before. He marked their progress from memory, recognizing the notches in the mountain peaks, the white granite walls that imposed themselves on the bend in the valley, and the boulder that looked like a giant nose.

They passed down into the foothills on the sixth day, and the riding became easier. They had made slow progress on account of Apaniaki. She was not yet showing, and riding would not pose significant danger, but Levi was still determined to minimize the stress of the venture as much as possible.

Where a time saving route that was more perilous presented itself, he chose instead to go the long way around. Where the rivers ran a bit too deep, they spent half a day looking for a shallow place to cross.

It took them about a day to work their way through the rolling hills that edged up against the mountains. Beyond them, the golden plain stretched as far as the eye could see, dotted here or there by a lonely stand of trees.

He hazarded a glance at Apaniaki, but his woman was leaning forward in the saddle, eyes forward, face set in eager yearning. She cut quite the picture sitting atop the little black mare. Spring breeze against her face, whipping strands of black hair into her eyes. Long lashes catching every tumble of the sun.

She looked at Levi and smiled. They rode on.

"Which way?" Levi asked.

Apaniaki pointed.

"As good as any," he said.

THEY HAD BEEN ON THE PRAIRIE FOR NO more than two days when they saw them, having gotten a late start on account of the cold morning. The sky was clear, but the temperature had dropped, and the wind blowing from the north was no longer warm.

It was second winter, those few weeks of bitter cold and heavy snows that came as Cold Maker made one last stand against the coming of spring. The figures on the far horizon were but shadows. Levi counted twelve of them. They were mounted. Sky lining themselves on the faraway ridge, their war bonnets and lances black against the blue sky.

"Can you make em out?" Levi asked.

Apaniaki shook her head.

Levi checked the powder in his Hawken and the pistols. Three guns against twelve. After his first shot, things would come to hand almost immediately.

They rode onward slowly, limiting the horses to a walk. The silhouettes did not move from the far ridge. Instead they shadowed them. Walking in perfect parallel no more than half a mile off. There was no use in running, the party was trying to make them lose their nerve, to startle them into running, the way a bear instigates a chase.

The prairie and the plain, at nearly all times, felt like an awful empty place. A man could go weeks without seeing hide nor hair of another human being, and it was in those times that he realized just how perilous a man alone was, for just about anything could ruin him. A broken leg or a lost horse, weather, predators, sickness. All leaving him no better than wolf bait. Man needed a tribe. People needed people. It's how we'd survived all these years.

Yet, because of that, there was a stubborn vanity in being the lone hunter; the man that walked the mountains with only his horse and a coyote to talk to. And that sort of life made a man mean, fighting mean, and awfully bad company when cornered. And now Levi was looking for his corner.

They rode onward with an eye towards their stalkers, and all the while, Levi looked for a place to make his stand.

The horsemen were taunting them. Testing their courage and baiting them into making a break for it. All predators chased when their prey fled, but only man took glee in triggering the flight. At least Levi imagined that to be so.

"Levi," Apaniaki said in a low shaky voice.

"Yeah?" Levi replied, eyes still set on the riders of the far hill.

"I love you," she said.

Forgetting the riders for but a moment, he looked at her. Her, with the misty eyes and the radiant skin.

"I love you," he said firmly. And as soon as he said it back, he knew their destinies were set. What they held he could not say, he only knew that every moment thereafter would be guided by the test of them.

Then ahead, where the land peeled out wide, and just at the foot of another hill, was a copse of trees. It was no more than a mile off, rising as an oasis. An island of cover in the vast sea of golden nothing.

"Run," Levi yelled, pointing at the far grove. And

Apaniaki kicked her horse to a gallop, while he followed behind her.

The horsemen gave a loud whoop, and came pouring down over the ridge towards them. The chase was on, and Levi whipped his mount forward, the big buffalo runner chewing up the land. The horse had much to give, and he had to rein him in to keep from outpacing Apaniaki. Together they flew over the plain, the horses running gallantly.

But the braves came fast, carried by the drumbeat of their hooves and the war-beat in their hearts.

A glance back and Levi saw them closing quickly. The copse of trees seemed no closer either, perhaps being larger and thus further off than he had first suspected.

Then Apaniaki's horse went down in a terrible tumble, throwing her several feet free even as the poor beast struggled to get back to his feet. Levi saw most of it out of the corner of his eye, and reacted quickly, losing no time to thought.

He wheeled Star Runner around, and galloped towards the place where Apaniaki had fallen. Her horse screamed in pain, a terrible sound, and Levi saw the white of its bone and the red of its flesh. A broken leg.

Apaniaki was up then, and running towards him.

He glanced at her, then back at the braves closing on them.

"Run!" he shouted again, pointing towards the the trees.

She stopped, dumbfounded at his command. But he'd already wheeled his horse away.

He nudged Star Runner forward into a lope towards the screaming Indians, pulling the big horse to a sudden stop. Then, trying to spot the leader, he shouldered the Hawken and took aim. He knew they had no chance to out run them, but perhaps killing their head man would break the warband's will, for Indians often fought on the strength of their leader's medicine.

They were a little less than 200 yards off when his finger closed around the trigger and the gun bucked. The brave he'd selected was torn free of his horse and sent somersaulting backwards off the back of his charging mount.

Then taking a short grip on the barrel of his empty rifle, he spurred Star Runner forwards toward the horde. They whooped and hollered as he closed. A flurry of arrows whined past, and he flattened himself onto the big horse's back.

Then, using the old musket as a club, he swung hard at the nearest. There was a terrible crack as maple stock met skull, and the warrior tumbled sideways off his painted mount.

Then another horse slammed into his, and Star Runner stumbled. Levi rode the horse down and stepped off him easy as can be letting the horse roll. He pulled both pistols free of their saddle holsters as the horse struggled back to its feet.

They were on him after that, and he leveled a pistol and fired point-blank into a brave that came riding in close and swinging a club. Another Indian stepped off his galloping pony and into a full sprint, hatchet raised, and looking to count coup. Levi emptied his second pistol into the man.

Then, a whirling circle of horse flesh, lean muscles, and singing lances. Levi grabbed a flashing lance and pulled its owner to the ground, swinging the tomahawk from his belt down on the man—a blow to the neck, hands grasping at its leaking blood, read feathers flashing in the morn.

Two braves slipped off their horses, lithe as leopards, knives in hand, and approached him. One tapped his friend, as if to tag him in, and then stepped backwards to watch the fight. It took Levi a moment to realize what was happening, for they had him dead to rights, regardless. But of all the races, only the Red Man had as much appetite for single combat as his White counterpart. Where others would happily turn a fight into murder by pure weight of numbers, the Indian tradition of counting coup made single combat a chance to cache songs and honor.

The other braves brought their horses to a standstill, making a mounted circle around the fighters. Whoops and hollers broke the great silence of the plain as they cheered their chosen hero on.

The brave lunged, and Levi knocked his plunging knife away, taking a swipe at the brave's face with the 'hawk. Then they were reset, both being cat quick, and back to circling. Again, the knife flashed, and this time Levi caught the hand that held it.

They were tumbling then, rolling around on the ground as they struggled for control of the gleaming weapon.

Levi let go of the 'hawk as the struggle thickened, its long handle and the close nature of the battle leaving no opportunity for leverage. His quarry was strong, one of the strongest he'd ever fought, and as they wrestled, he felt no give in the man. He had two hands around the braves wrist when he felt knuckles and a flutter of punches target his kidneys.

The pain and adrenaline spurred creative action, and Levi slammed a downward elbow into the brave's gut.

The knife came free as the lone warrior seized up breathless. Levi caught up the knife and brought it high and ready to stab.

But white hot pain stayed his hand. He dropped the knife, or rather, it was thrown from his hand, he could not tell which, and in its place was the shaft of an arrow. Slick with his own blood, and buried up to the feathers in the back of his hand.

He whirled around then, desperate to place eyes on his attacker, more angry at the intervention than the arrow through his palm.

One of the warriors stood his horse laughing. His war bonnet a bright angry red and white, the bottom half of his face painted the same color. In the man's hands was a gleaming bow, made of horn, and polished to a smooth icy finish, limbs wrapped in snakeskin, and from its handle hung the same snake's dried rattle. It was then that Levi recognized this man as the leader of the band, and not the brave that he'd shot with the Hawken.

Another warrior grabbed his opposite arm, and yet another stepped forward, striking a blow across his face that made his head ring, and like that, honor and coup was all but forgotten.

Levi dropped to his knees, and felt fingers curl around his own scalp lock as his head and neck were thrust violently forward. Frantically, he tried to break free of the arms that gripped him, but to no avail.

He'd made peace with losing his hair long ago, but he was not one to die without fighting. To be slaughtered like a deer or a sheep or a goat.

"STOP!" a woman cried out—it was Apaniaki. She had returned, but from where he did not know, for he'd lost track of her during the fighting. The damn woman. "Let him live and I will go with you willingly," she said. The words were in her tongue, but Levi could make them out.

The laughing brave before him held out a leveled

hand to stay his brothers. Then, he swung down from his horse.

Levi's heart caught in his throat, and he cursed Apaniaki in that moment. Maybe she had saved him, maybe she had not. Regardless, the cost was too great a thing for him to bear. It was the very thing he'd been willing to die for, her freedom, and the chance his child may survive to live among the same mountains he'd given his heart to.

The brave grabbed Apaniaki roughly by the arm and dragged her forward into view.

"Kill him and I die," she said. She brandished a knife, gripping it with both hands, its tip pressed against her own bosom, white knuckles decorating its handle.

The brave before him looked at her, and he seemed to glare, but then his gaze softened. Something of a plan, or a plot, flashed across his face, and he broke into a smile.

He barked orders that Levi could not understand.

One of them brought Star Runner to the brave, and it was in that moment that Levi recognized him as its rightful owner.

THE ONE SHE HAD CALLED LARGE TEETH told Apaniaki that they would not kill him, but that they should let the gods decide, and this seemed enough for her, for she relaxed her grip on the knife. Levi barely made this out, though his grasp on the language was still rudimentary

The braves dragged him backwards then, and it took four of them to do so, even as he fought against them. They snapped two lances over their knees, and taking a stone up from the earth, used it as a hammer to pound their newly made stakes into the ground making four points of a square.

They slammed him backwards and taking rawhide cords, bound him hand and foot, spread eagle on his back. They pulled the cords tight, so tight they bit his wrists. Then they poured water on them, and pulled them even tighter, knowing that they would tighten as they dried.

The one called Large Teeth loaded Apaniaki onto the back of Star Runner, and then climbed up behind her. The brave smiled at him, a big menacing smile. He was victorious, and Levi was all but dead. Left as bait for the buzzards, or the bears, or whatever found him first, assuming the sun didn't have time to receive its sacrifice.

With whoops and hollers they were gone, and when their dust settled, all that was left was a clear blue sky. Two buzzards already circled high above. His hands lost feeling, and his tongue swelled prematurely.

CHAPTER 22
RUINS

SHE WOULD NOT LET LARGE TEETH OR ANY OF the others see her pain. She would not allow them the pleasure of gloating. She would go straight away to her father and convince him to go after Levi. She had decided these things, sworn to them, and repeated them back to herself over and over again, even as the band of warriors escorted her back home.

Large Teeth rode forward of her, with a brilliant war bonnet made of eagle feathers crowning his head. His shoulders were wide under the buffalo hide coat that draped them, and the bottom of it spilled out over his black horse's rump.

He turned in the saddle, and grinned at her, his mouth wide and teeth gleaming. He had wolfish eyes that had always set her on edge, but now they scared her, ravenous as they were. They were searching eyes, that seemed to take without asking, that took whatever they laid upon.

She shifted her eyes and chin proudly. He would never have her, for she was Levi's only. Her father would help her, for though he was stubborn, he loved her dearly. She knew that, and she did not doubt it.

She had asked for very little from her father. She had been grateful to him in both want and plenty, but now she would throw herself at his feet and beg him for this one heart's desire. Black Crow would not turn her away.

The thought of his name stirred up longing in her. She missed him. She had missed his laugh, and the stern loving look that always made her feel safe when she was scared. She missed seeing him and Fox Kitten Woman warm by the fire, content to stare into each other's eyes and laugh together, even after all these years. It was her father's fault she'd fell so quickly to love's poison. It was he who had taught her to love with her whole heart, even as she ran from it.

She thought back to the story he'd told her about Singing Woman, and the loss of his first child, and how overwhelmed with grief and anger he'd been. She'd understood the story then, felt it even, but now it grasped her heart with the surreal knowing that only personal experience could bring.

She feared for Levi, and she feared for her baby.

A thought came to her then, from outside of her, a thought so startling that a chill passed over her. If Levi died, she would have to marry Large Teeth. The pregnancy was early enough that she could try to pass the baby off as his. If she didn't, then what? Raise a *bastard half-breed*. The words had again come from outside of her, for she had never thought of such a phrase, and the voice that the words came riding on was Shining Feathers', the old woman without a nose.

"Save your tears little one, for if you shed them all now, you will have none when they are needed," the old ugly woman had cackled.

Tears broke from their dams, and traveled down

Apaniaki's cheeks, cutting clean trails through the dust and grime that covered her face. Apaniaki sat in her despair for but a moment, the world narrowing, blurring even. She felt the horse move beneath her, rhythmically, as the warm breeze tickled her neck. Then she wiped her face, and focused her eyes ahead, forcing the thoughts, the voices, and the memories away from her.

They traveled North for about a day, and then coming to a river, turned West and followed it up into the rolling hills. On the second day, the familiar rows of white lodges and their corresponding fingers of smoke appeared ahead of them, hidden away at the foot of a hill.

She had despaired for Levi, tied up, and staked out as he was, but she was grateful that he had been left alive. That would not be his end for he was too strong, and the mountains, and even the gods seemed to be his ally. Already she believed that he had found a way loose of his bindings.

The camp of her people looked smaller than usual, certainly smaller than she remembered it. She wondered then if this was growing up. If this was that time Fox Kitten Woman had spoken of, when things encountered in childhood shrank in size and danger. When the world lost its big blossoming shine, and the cold smallness of reality made itself known. That was becoming a woman. That was the loss that came with knowing love.

When they were no more than half a mile away from the small camp, Apaniaki could wait no longer. She needed to see Black Crow. She glanced at Large Teeth, who sat all but oblivious to her, and then threw her legs wide, slamming her heels into the sides of the little black, kicking him to an immediate gallop.

She rode fast, taking a grip on the rawhide reins, and didn't pull up until she was already inside the row of lodges. As the horse slid to a stop, she glided off his back, giving one furtive glance backwards toward Large Teeth and his men. She was surprised they had not followed her.

She felt a hand on her arm, and recognized the woman as Singing Bird, one of her old friends. Singing Bird's eyes shone with shock and surprise at her sudden homecoming, but Apaniaki shoved the girl away.

She ran forward towards the center of the small encampment, her eyes searching for the markings of her father's lodge, until at last, she found it. Its doorway still guarded by two big black painted Crows, each facing each other. Its top striped the way the Crow had shown him long ago.

"Father," she called, pushing her way inside. The lodge was dark, and it took a moment for her eyes to adjust.

Then she saw a figure sitting on the opposite wall —him.

"Apaniaki," The figure said.

It wasn't him though.

It was the voice of a woman. "Oh, Apaniaki," Fox Kitten Woman cried out. The figure rushed to her, throwing herself in Apaniaki's arms, and having no sooner done so, broke down weeping.

"Where is Father?" Apaniaki asked desperately, "I must talk to him."

But the woman did not stop her uncontrollable sobbing. Apaniaki struggled beneath the weight of Fox Kitten Woman, who now clasped her tightly.

Finally, Apaniaki managed to break free of her grasp and holding her at arm's length asked again, "Where is father?"

The woman's slender frame trembled and convulsed. "He is... gone," the weeping woman replied.

"Where?" Apaniaki asked. "When did he go? I need to see him." She gave Fox Kitten Woman a small shake, and had no sooner asked the questions, when a second possibility revealed itself to her, one that would explain the woman racked with sorrow... "No, it cannot be," Apaniaki gasped the words.

Her Mother nodded, her deep brown eyes cloudy with grief.

Apaniaki squinted at the woman's puffy face, unwilling to believe it, "Tell me he is alive, Fox Kitten Woman."

In that moment, it seemed to take all the energy the old woman could muster to shake her head slowly from side to side.

Apaniaki slid to her knees then, crumpling into a pile that brought the old woman down with her, and they cried loudly into each other's arms.

SHE STOOD ON THE EDGE OF THE encampment, in the place where Red Beaver's lodge should be. Instead, there was nothing but black ash, and a terrible scar in the earth.

"I'm sorry Apaniaki," Large Teeth said from behind her. "I didn't know how to tell you."

"How did it happen?" she asked, not moving her eyes from the horrible place.

"The white scabs sickness. The great evil," Large Teeth said slowly. "It swept through the camp. Red Beaver took care of the sick as best he could, but he could only do so much. Then evil took him as well. We lost many."

"But my father already had the scars from the

great evil... from when he first found me," Apaniaki said. "He had told me the evil could not touch him again."

"Your father did not die from the sickness."

"How, then?"

"A bear," Large Teeth said. "High up in the mountains, we went hunting the great bear that we might kill him and receive some of his strength."

"But why?" Apaniaki asked.

"Your father grew worried about the band," he continued. "Our numbers were made low by the Long Knives' evil, by the sickness. He said we needed strength for the summer ahead. That the Parted Hairs would attack us if they saw us so weak."

"Why did you not help him?"

"I tried, but Bear was too quick," Large Teeth said. "He snatched him up and dragged him off into the woods."

"And you did not go after him?" she asked. The words came out breathlessly, exasperated—angry.

"I could not find him," Large Teeth said. "The great Bear disappeared; and he left no tracks."

"Go from me," Apaniaki cried. "You lie."

"Apaniaki, there is more," Large Teeth said. "That night, after the bear had taken him. Black Crow came to me in a dream. He said he was on his way to the sand hills. He told me to find you, and to bring you back to our people."

Apaniaki shook in anger at his words. "Tell me then," she said, turning at last to face him. "Who will be Chief now that my father is gone?"

"I am already Chief," Large Teeth said. "The council chose me. They must still vote at the council of All the People, when the big bands meet. But for now, I am Chief, as the people have lost many warriors, old and young."

The air seemed to thicken around her, even as she gasped for breath. Her vision narrowed, and her head grew faint, as every plan she'd conceived of, every chance to rescue Levi was wrested from her hands, not by Large Teeth, but by fate and the gods themselves.

She slumped to the ground. Large Teeth knelt next to her.

"Go away," she said softly.

As he slunk away, she clutched her knees to her chest tightly and began to rock back and forth.

How could this happen? How had she had no warning? No dream? She cried then, heavy sobs, that racked her whole body and she cried out to the One Above that he might set all of this right.

She stayed like that for a long time, hands outstretched, and pleading with the One Above that he might hear her sorrow. That he might turn back the great wheel of time and choose another thread for her life.

She cried loudly, that the whole camp might hear her prayers. That they might all bear witness to some small portion of her misery. Then, when she had no more to give, she collapsed backwards, and hugged her knees even tighter to her body, so tight that she might not be torn apart by the great heaving grief that so bodily tortured her. She lay there all night, soaked in pain, and the cold had no effect on her, for she was already as if one of the dead.

She awoke in the morning, to the pinks and grays of a new morn, and the gentle touch of Fox Kitten Woman.

"Shhh," the old woman whispered. "Come back with me little one."

Gently, Fox Kitten Woman tugged her upwards, and Apaniaki stumbled to her feet.

As the woman guided her back through the encampment, Apaniaki walked on wooden feet. Her feet, her hands, her body were all unfamiliar to her now, even as were all of the things outside of her. She was numb.

Inside her father's lodge, she sat down gracelessly, and fell at once to her side. She did not sleep. She merely stared at the hide wall in front of her.

CHAPTER 23
ANTI-LIFE

THE CORDS STRETCHED TIGHT, LIGHTING each of his limbs in a searing pain matched only by the corresponding stiffness in his joints. His wrists had started to bleed, and he had long since lost feeling in his fingers. His thumbs looked blue and black, both from loss of blood flow but also bruising.

Levi's tongue had swollen from thirst, and his lips had begun to crack, and his mouth tasted copper, and the newly hatched spring sun grew in power.

As it was spring, it took a long time for the sun to have its way with him, which was perhaps worse than being staked out in the middle of a dreadful summer. For this was death by slow and soothing warmth. Death from the inside out, as his body slowly dehydrated.

To die in the middle of winter was in some ways the original lot cast for every man. The fated end every human baby had planned for them, unless they changed their lot through virtue or warfare. To die in summer, a bloody death, while soaked in sweat and hate, was a death saved only for the most diligent fighters. To die in the autumn, seemed to mark a life well lived, a fitting and noble end—a sign that God was merciful and kind. But a death like this, staked helplessly under a maternal sun, with daffodils blooming among soft new shoots of green grass, and the birds singing happy songs, seemed a death that had been colluded to. A death that fates and enemies had planned.

Already several black vultures circled high above, riding the warm winds and counting away the hours. Levi had never been a hopeless man. He had at times been guilty of a sour disposition, and perhaps even a dour outlook on the comings and goings of man, but he had never forgotten the power of a proud look, an even disposition, and the dignity of bright shiny eyes. But now, with his woman and his child stolen from him, and left to rot from within, he despaired.

He could not help but reason that he had misstepped. Forces above his knowing had gathered to instruct him in some lesson that he did not grasp. The dark star of his birth, feeling spurned, had no doubt taken to righting the order of things. He blamed himself for the situation, for listening to Apaniaki, for believing that that her people would treat them honorably. But perhaps his error began earlier than that, perhaps it began with giving any credence whatsoever to the superstitious ramblings of an Old Indian.

Or maybe it was all quite bullshit. All of it, he reasoned. The thought gave him some small comfort; some consolation in a fight well fought. Maybe things just happened. Bodies were set on a path of collision and driven only by survival and the chance for breeding. Was this not the thing called love? Was not the whole of Man's body dedicated to such a purpose? Was this not truth, and the whole of it, the essence of existence. Man's whole design, from his hip to shoulder, meant for the defense of his bitch and his territory, like some wild dog that roamed the black wood, destined to die in a test of hierarchy; its only legacy the bright white jagged mouths of the pups it had whelped.

Levi tested the cords once more, but the only thing that gave was the flesh on his wrists.

The sun hung high in the sky, and by late afternoon the first whisps of clouds began to blow past. He lay there watching the cotton clouds chase the vultures away. They gave up their post when the thermals disappeared, no doubt settling somewhere close by. He prayed that the clouds would bring with them a spring rain. Perhaps enough to soak the rawhide cords and turn the earth to mud beneath the stakes that held him.

And indeed, rain came just before sunset. A quick shower that soaked him to the bone. The rawhide bands, newly wet, gave his hands a small bit of relief. Catching rain in his open mouth helped soothe his swollen tongue. But as the sun disappeared behind its black horizon, the temperature dropped significantly. He lay shivering in the black of night, the stars overhead being little comfort for the sounds around him. Some way off he heard a wolf howl, a sound that made his blood run cold, bound defenseless as he was. Every scratch and titter turned field mice into specter.

There was a point in the night where he had grown so cold, and sore, and his bones ached so thoroughly that he began to sing. He did not remember any hymns, nor songs from his childhood really, and could only manage to call up a single river shanty from his time aboard the keelboat. He sang loud and deep, from the very bottom of his chest so that the vibration of it all both soothed his mind and warmed his core.

Missouri, she's a mighty river.
Away, you rolling river.
The redskins' camp lies on its borders.
Ah-ha, I'm bound away, 'Cross the wide Missouri.
Oh! John Skenandoa
The white man loved the Indian maiden,
Away, you rolling river.
With notions his canoe was laden.
Ah-ha, I'm bound away, 'Cross the wide Missouri.
Oh! John Skenandoa...

Long into the night Levi sang, over and over again, concentrating on the words in his chest, until both gave out, and the old shanty was nothing more than a hoarse whisper. He fell asleep sometime in the morning, right as dawn's rosy fingers pulled back the black horizon and rose from her covering.

HE WOKE TO A FLURRY OF DUST AND WINGS. The sun blinded him, and his head pounded from lack of water. Staring at him, but a few inches away from his face, was an old buzzard. Its black dusty skin hanging in loose folds from its head. Its beak razor sharp, cracked and jagged. Black eyes flicked across Levi's body. Deep, soulless eyes, that searched for death in all its forms and nothing else.

The bird gave a small croak as it tilted its head sideways.

"Go away, git," Levi tried to shout, but the words that came out were anything but audible.

He grunted and groaned at the bird, shaking his head harshly at the great flying beast, but it made no move away from him.

Then the sun was blotted by quick shadow as the bird's companions landed nearby. They hopped around, rasping and muttering among themselves in some alien tongue. Each one cocking its head sideways at different intervals. One ruffled its feathers sending up a plume of dust, and another attacked its fellow for no apparent reason.

The true dread of the creatures lay in their ugliness, the entirety of their character being borne out in their appearance. No noble beast could ever be so ugly. The wolf, even in all of its terror, was still beautiful, with its coarse black fur, amber eyes, and power in its haunches. Or the lithe cougar, that slank around in a coat spun from soft gold. But here was the carrion eater, with its dusty barren eyes, and its bald, naked head, unable as it was to make its own kill. Here was the one that waited, the plotter, the patient harbinger of death ill won—the anti-life.

The vultures approached him slowly, hopping forward on scaled talons, even as their sharp murmuring reached a crescendo. They would go for the soft parts first. His eyes and his lips, and then they would work on the other end, picking at his groin, working their way towards the middle until they could slide their naked head up inside his chest cavity and steal away his steaming organs.

A black beak shot toward his face, and he turned his head away, the back of his skull erupting in pain. The bird jumped backwards then, put off by the fact that its meal was still moving, and unable even now to risk conflict. The other birds danced backwards, purring to themselves, communicating their distrust and envy through clicks and gurgles.

Fear had grasped all of Levi at this point, and that sharp drug, fear, lit what was left of his body on electric fire. He heaved against the bindings, but they only cut deeper. The pain was fuel to him, and he decided then that it was better to bleed out than watch these brutal creatures pick at him alive.

Then he heard a yelp, and again, like so many times before, that tan blur he knew as Loki had arrived to rescue him. The coyote came in barking and yipping, his jaws snapping at the buzzards. And they fled to the skies, beating the air with great heavy wings. Levi watched as the demons departed to again spin circles above him.

Loki approached him then. His yellow eyes curious as to why Levi had not yet escaped his predicament. Levi motioned his head towards the bindings and muttered a command for the dog to free him, hoping that the loyal creature would chew through his corded bonds. But the Coyote just looked at him blankly. Too ignorant to realize his potential usefulness.

The dog lay down next to Levi, resting his head gently on the man's stomach.

Levi pleaded with the dog throughout the day, trying to convince him to chew through the cords. At one point, the coyote even got up and licked his wrists, as if to soothe his wounds.

It was afternoon when Levi gave up. He melted into the ground, letting his head rest, and releasing all the tension from his body. His neck was sore from straining.

Loki stared at him from a few feet away, now curled up and trying to nap. The sun began to sink lower in the sky, and Levi resigned himself to death. He would not make it through another night. He was too weak. The cold would take him, and he would slip into oblivion.

Loki perked his ears and raised his head, growling low. Levi twisted his head, this way and that, trying to see what approached. There was movement. A scuffle of feet.

Loki rose, pinning his ears back and showing his teeth, even as the noise in his throat grew tremulously.

Then at last, a silhouette stood above him. That of a man. He was nothing but shadow, the sun being so bright behind him. Levi recognized him as Death come to collect its bounty.

CHAPTER 24
THE PROPOSAL

APANIAKI HAD NOT NOTICED THEM WHEN she'd first approached the camp, the black scars where the tents of the sick had been burnt in place. At least half of the band had seemingly perished. A great sadness filled all of the remainder. Even the children did not laugh or play the way she remembered. Some of them had lost both parents and had then moved in with an uncle or relative when possible. Others, who had just escaped adolescence, but had not yet married, now lived in lodges of their own, populated only by themselves. Which was a lonely thing, and something the people were not used to.

She sat outside of her father's lodge, cross-legged, elbow on knee, and chin in hand. She twirled a long piece of dried grass around her other hand, watching it go around and around.

The sun felt good on her face and warmed the backs of her arms. The sky was made of blue crystal and completely cloudless. She could not remember a sky ever being so cloudless. The wind blew down off the mountains, and did not howl, or groan, or even whisper. It moved silently over the land, leaving only the gentle sway of the grass and flutter in the trees as witness. She imagined Levi next to her, sitting silently, with his brooding look of quiet concern. He had only ever smiled at her. At all other times, his face had been set hardened, eyes forward and always scanning.

She had never seen him mad. Never seen him agitated or frustrated. Never even worried or fearful. Even when she had come back in order to save him, he had not seemed afraid, but rather committed. His eyes had shone like a badger's.

She remembered when Black Crow had shown her the wolves they had trapped in a pit one winter. They had dug a sort of pit and then erected a pyramidal structure over it from logs taken nearby. The top of the pyramid was left open, and a bait carcass dropped inside.

The wolves, smelling the bait carcass would climb up the sides of the trap and drop down within, but were unable to get back out. The wolves had snarled at them, and snapped their jaws, pacing the walls of the pit and looking for escape, but even as proud as they were, she had seen the fear in their eyes. The fear that all intelligent animals were imbued with.

She also remembered stumbling upon a badger that was caught in one of the Long Knives' traps. He had chewed almost the whole way through his own leg, and his eyes shone not with fear at her approach, but utter aggression. That was the look that she had seen in Levi's eyes.

She felt her own eyes begin to water, but she swallowed hard and clinched her jaw. She had sworn off shedding more tears. She would be proud now, like Levi, and like her father. She would not give more tears, for every time she cried, she felt worse than the last time. Like more of herself had disappeared.

Large Teeth appeared in the distance. His lean figure looking small when compared to the sky behind him. He was walking towards her.

She hated him. Hated his manner. His walk. His every tick and movement.

He sat down next to her and said nothing.

She hated him even more in that moment, for his presumption, his steadfast pursuit—for the small pity she couldn't help but feel for him. He had killed Levi. Killed him in the most awful way possible, and still he was here, simpering for her affection.

She started crying then. The tears that she had choked down just a minute earlier bubbling back up for sudden release.

She felt a gentle hand on her leg. A comforting hand.

Her blood ran cold. The tears dried up, and she snapped her eyes first to him, and then to his hand.

"Do not touch me," she said. "Do not come near me."

Large Teeth withdrew his hand, and his eyes filled with a sudden hate. She'd never seen that look in him before, the sudden spite, the malevolence—the evil.

It scared her, but she held his look. Matched it even. The tears stopped, replaced by a deep roiling hatred.

"Two days," he said. "We will be married. Do not make trouble. Do not try to escape. It is as Black Crow wished. The gods have made their choice. The people need their Medicine Woman, and they need a Chief. Together, we will make them strong again."

He picked himself up then and walked off. He did not look back.

CHAPTER 25
RESURRECTION

It was not death that had come to collect him. It was the Old Man. Within minutes, the dark figure had slashed through the rawhide bindings that had held Levi tied to the earth and sat cradling him in his arms.

He gave him a sip of water from the leather water skin that hung at his side.

"Did you miss me, Long Knife?" the Old Man asked.

Levi stared up at the wrinkled face of his savior through swollen slits. Levi's lips were cracked, and the skin of his face drawn tight and gaunt ahead of looming death. Slowly blood returned to his four limbs, lighting them up with an incredible fire.

After a while of this, the Old Man gently set Levi up so that he could sit under his own strength. Loki sat nearby, watching the Old Man's movements closely, ever on guard for a sudden attack or a sign that meant danger to his friend. Once the Old Man stumbled while gathering buffalo chips, and Loki made a small lunge at him, hackles raised, his upper lip quivering beneath the growl in his throat.

Having gathered the chips, the Old Man built a fire, and Levi warmed himself by its crackling flame. It was nearly sundown, and the temperature was again starting to drop, but it was still nice out. The sky was cloudless, and the sunset was just a gradual change from blue to deep purple. The Old Man had hobbled his horse a little way off, and Levi was surprised to see his mule, Jack Wagon, hobbled next to him.

"I found him after I left you," the Old Man said, sitting down beside the fire.

"But how'd you find me?" Levi asked.

The Old Man pointed a finger towards the sky. High above them, the buzzards still circled, marking them as easy prey for miles.

Levi grunted, and the Old Man handed him a bit of jerked venison from the small leather meat pouch at his side. He was a grizzled figure, short gray hairs growing out of the chin that he'd long since given up plucking. His silver hair pulled backwards into a knotted braid. Crow's feet pulled the edges of his sun hardened face sideways, and his mouth seemed set in a permanent frown.

The fire felt good, and Levi was happy to see the Old Man, even if he was still a bit surprised that he was alive.

"You kill Black Crow yet?" Levi asked, half joking.

"No." The Old Man said, scowling. "I holed up for the winter. A very long winter. I was on my way back down when I found you."

"Why you want to kill him so bad?" Levi asked.

The Old Man took his tobacco pipe out of his bag and packed it full. Levi reached over and lit it with a stick from the fire. The Old Man puffed it to life.

"It is my end," the Old Man finally said. "Many seasons, many sleeps, the Lakota and the Piikani were at peace. We met to celebrate the coming together of our people. This, after a particularly long period of fighting.

"I was young then, and ready to take a wife. I had been promised to a woman named Singing Girl. She was very lovely, but she did not see me. When our peoples met for the celebration, she ran away with the Piikani. The one they called Black Crow.

"This brought me great dishonor for a long time, often the others would say I was the one who gave his girl away. For a time, I was even called Stolen Girl. This was a name I swore to change. I led a raid against Blackfoot after that, and became a War Chief for the People. The time of peace came to an end. But I never found or saw Singing Girl again, and never met Black Crow in battle."

"You ever think that maybe she was happy?" Levi asked, taking the pipe from the Old Man.

"Does it matter?" the Old Man asked. "She was mine. She was promised to me by her father."

"But did you love her?" Levi asked.

The Old Man paused at that, thinking for a moment, and then he said, "What is love if not respect. I would have killed her for breaking the oath, as was my right."

"A bit stiff for a filly you didn't even love," Levi said.

"It is a matter of word. Of bond. If one's woman cannot remain loyal to him, how are the men he must lead in battle to be loyal. How does a tribe function if everyone does what they want?"

"Maybe," Levi said. "Did you ever marry?"

"I did," the Old Man said. "She died four seasons ago."

"So then why?" Levi asked.

"Because I must finish what was started," the Old Man replied.

"Your people do not do this?" the Old Man asked.

"Do what?" Levi asked.

"Arrange marriage?" the Old Man said.

"I suppose we do. Some of us. It's common enough I suppose, but I think we try to leave room for a marriage of beauty. And we certainly don't kill no one for eloping."

"We leave room for beauty—for love," the Old Man said. "Most pick their own wives, they chase each other all of childhood. But sometimes, the old ones know better. Sometimes it does not matter what one wants, only what must happen, for the good of the tribe. And once those decisions are made, we expect our women to be loyal."

"But all this time, all these years," Levi said, "why not just make peace with the man?"

"Maybe," the Old Man grinned at the thought of that. "Or maybe not, I have thought of that day for too long. I have had a vision of my end. It is after that fight."

"And you are successful?"

"I am," the Old Man said. "But so is he."

"Yeah," said Levi. "I suppose we are on two different paths then, huh."

"Maybe," the Old Man said. "Maybe it is the same. You are good man, even though you ride with the trickster."

LEVI FELL ASLEEP AFTER THAT. EXHAUSTED from his time by the fire, his head buzzing slightly from the tobacco he'd imbibed. He felt damn good, all things considered. Oh, he was a mess alright. His wrists were all torn up, and his muscles stretched and sore. His shoulders feeling like they'd been stomped on by a herd of a hundred wild horses. But he wasn't thirsty, and his belly was full, and the tobacco had soothed his spirit as much as it calmed his head, even as it filled his mouth with comforting ash.

Sometime in the night, a horse snorted.

Levi woke to the sound. Then he heard a flurry of footsteps, and a grunt. The Old Man was no longer next to him. Levi pulled himself to his feet, slowly, for he was still stiff, and grabbed a flaming brand from the fire.

Then he heard another grunt, and a flutter of activity. He'd just started towards the noise, when the Old Man was thrown backwards out of the darkness and fell into the light of the fire. Then from the darkness came his attacker, an Indian just as old.

Levi started towards the charging man, but his friend yelled no.

"He is mine," the Old Man said. "It is Black Crow."

Levi took a step back, as the charging Indian jumped on the downed Old Man.

The two of them tumbled through the fire, throwing sparks everywhere as they grappled for top position. The Old Man was victorious. Having mounted his mortal enemy and latched fragile hands around the Chief's neck.

Levi circled them then, looking on as if both judge and referee. Black Crow heaved his hips, bucking the Old Man from his place straddled across him. With a quick roll, Black Crow was back on his feet.

The two circled then, like two old bull elk, far beyond their years, returned to the same valley where they were born, ready to settle their old rotten score. There was still tremendous strength in the old men, yet it was faltering quickly, each wayward blow landing more softly then the last.

Levi could hear their breath turn to wheezing, but still the two old dogs tried to fight. They tumbled and clawed at each other, gasping for breath, and grunting loudly.

Levi sat down and watched as the two tussled. He pulled the pipe from the Old Man's bag and lit it. As he puffed it, he watched the slim fingers of smoke curl upward. Beyond the barrel of the pipe, the two figures had finally reached a standstill. Both on their knees, facing each other, Black Crow having wrapped up the Old Man's arms in a sort of clinch.

With the last of his strength, the Old Man heaved Black Crow off him, and they both fell backwards, landing flat on their backs, where they lay with mouths open, sucking air like two fish that had landed themselves in the bottom of a keelboat.

Levi approached the two slowly, and then kneeling down next to Black Crow, gave him the pipe. The old chief looked from Levi then back to the pipe with eyes that were still bright, and pushed himself up onto an elbow. A trickle of blood ran from his nose into his mouth, which he wiped on a dirty buckskin sleeve. He took the pipe from Levi and took a long puff, blowing smoke slowly out.

The Old Man, upon seeing this, struggled to his knees, angered at the fact that Levi had not only passed the pipe to Black Crow before him, but had let him smoke from his own pipe at all. The Old Man snatched the pipe from Black Crows hands and quickly drew an even longer puff. He'd barely done so, when his eyes went wide, and he started choking on the smoke after trying to exhale it at once.

Levi started laughing then, "That's right Old Man. You smoked together. You just made peace."

The Old Man glared at Levi, and stood up defiantly. He threw the pipe harshly into the lap of Black Crow.

"But my vision," the Old Man started. "My death must be—"

"—To hell with your vision," Levi shouted. He was standing now. Every bit of his six feet towering over the Old Man, and the seated chief. "Dream this, dream that. Curses. Superstitions. I'm fucking sick of it." Levi put a finger in the Old Man's face. "Now you sit down, and you make peace. And I don't want to hear anything more about spirit animals or will-o'-wisps that made you do it. And after that we are going to ride to HIS camp"—Levi snapped his finger towards Black Crow—"and I will have my wife back, and the hair of the one that took her."

Slowly, Old Man looked from Levi back to Black Crow, then his face softened, and all the tension fell from his shoulders.

He shrugged and muttered in disbelief, "I have made peace. I have been tricked into making peace."

Levi extended Black Crow an arm and hauled him up to his feet.

He guided Apaniaki's father to a place by the fire and saw then for the first time that the fight had not been totally fair. The old Chief had a makeshift splint on his leg, and his buckskin pants were now damp and red with blood from whatever wound had been torn open.

The Chief winced as Levi set him down.

"What happened?" Levi asked.

"It does not matter," Black Crow said. "Where is my daughter. Where is Apaniaki."

Levi sat back on his haunches, and replied, "Large Teeth took her. We were on our way back to ask your blessing, that we might marry. He ambushed us, tied me down, and staked me out."

"She cannot marry him. It must be stopped. He has deceived me for the last time."

"Deceived you?" Levi asked.

"Yes," Black Crow said. "He drew me out to the mountains, fearing that I had guessed the evil that he brought down upon us."

"What evil?" Levi asked.

"The white scabs sickness. He attacked the Long Knives, the ones much like yourself, when Cold Maker had warned against it."

"The sickness passed through the camp, and many died. Large Teeth himself became sick, but somehow, he survived.

"Before Red Beaver, our medicine man passed, he told me of the warning. He said that Large Teeth had attacked the Long Knives, and this is why the evil had come to us. When I had gone to confront him, he jumped me. He was taking me high into the mountains to kill me, when I escaped."

"What happened to your leg?" Levi asked.

"After I made my escape, I fell down a rocky cliff. I broke it. But it only slowed me a little, for I put the splint on it, and set it, and was returning to the tribe, when I saw the buzzards circling. When I crept closer, I found you and the Old Man. I did not know it was you, but I saw the horses, and so I waited until nightfall that I might steal one," Black Crow said. Then he motioned at the Old Man, and said, "You are lucky he is not also a Long Knife, otherwise I would have been successful."

At this the Old Man chuckled.

Black Crow turned back to Levi and said, "So you want to marry my daughter?"

"Yes," Levi said.

"And you go after her tomorrow?" asked Black Crow.

Levi nodded.

"Good. Then you may have her but you must do one thing for me."

"Anything," Levi said.

"You must save him for me."

Levi thought for a long moment. Then at last he said, "You may have the killing blow, but I get everything that comes before."

"Good," Black Crow said. And with that, the old chief shifted his position downward, and closed his eyes.

CHAPTER 26
REVENGE

LARGE TEETH WOKE EARLY IN THE MORNING, the fire in his lodge having died out the night before. He stirred the coals, and piled more wood on top, his breath blowing clouds in the early morning chill. After he'd put more wood on the fire, he blew softly on the coals and gave new life to the flames.

He heard movement outside, and then a horse whinnied, while another answered. They were here. The Band of the Four Winds, their brother tribe. Their Chief, Light Owl, and Medicine Man had come to perform the marriage ceremony and give Large Teeth their blessing for Chief. He would of course still have to go up before the tribal council this summer, at the great meeting, but with Light Owl's blessing, he would be chief until then.

Large Teeth pulled on his moccasins and yanked their rawhide thongs tight, tying them off around the top and then tucking them inside. He struggled to his feet, still tired, from a restless night's sleep.

He had not slept well. He had often been visited in the night by Spotted Locust, but now he brought with him Black Crow, and Red Beaver. They appeared in his dreams, chastising him for the path he had followed. Even the old snake woman who had first given him her medicine no longer visited. He had found her once, at least two moons back, with her back turned to him, and crying. She'd told him that she was ashamed. That he had brought dishonor to the snake and his medicine. Snake had always been a friend of the people, but now they would look on him with disdain.

Large Teeth pulled open the flap to his lodge and stepped outside. Already, the camp was moving with the early morning chores. Others were greeting Light Owl and Rains Hard Man, the Four Winds Band's Medicine Man. Large Teeth dried off sweaty palms and walked towards the two elders. They both greeted him with smiles and approving nods.

"Large Teeth," said Light Owl, "it is good to see you again. Last time I did so, I do not remember you being so grown."

"That was three summers ago," Large Teeth said. "Much has changed since then. But come, let us talk in my lodge."

With that Large Teeth led the two elders to his lodge and showed them to a place by his fire. He sat down and took out his own pipe that they may smoke.

"It is not good that a Chief has no woman to bring him his pipe," Light Owl said.

Rains Hard Man nodded along, his stony expression remaining unchanged.

"Today, that changes though," Large Teeth said happily, and at that Light Owl smiled.

"You are very young," Light Owl said. "But it is good that your band has you to lead them. We do not always know what the Great Ones have planned for us, but we can take heart in the fact that there will always be those fit to lead with strength and courage."

Large Teeth nodded slowly, saying nothing. He puffed the pipe, and passed it to Light Owl, who took a long draw himself before passing it to Rains Hard Man.

They talked then of the many woes that Large Teeth's band had suffered, from the raid of the Crows that had stolen Apaniaki, to the death of Black Crow and Red Beaver, and then about the great sickness, which was only whispered about that they might not raise the evil again.

It was mid-morning when the drums for the ceremony started beating. Light Owl, having grown tired of talking, pushed himself to his feet, and wished Large Teeth well.

"After the ceremony, I shall give you my blessing as Chief," he said, and with that, he departed the lodge.

Steals Many Horses, who had been waiting patiently, entered afterwards, carrying the ceremonial shirt that Little Bird Woman had made. It was made of otter skin and extremely soft, decorated with red and blue quills and copper beads. Large Teeth struggled out of his buckskins, and pulled the shirt on, leaving it open in the front so that his chest and abdomen were left exposed. Steals Many Horses draped a shell necklace over the head of his friend, and fixed the ceremonial feathers threaded into his hair.

When he was ready, Steals Many Horses stepped outside, and went to talk to Fox Kitten Woman, who confirmed that Apaniaki was also ready.

APANIAKI STOOD IN FRONT OF LARGE TEETH. Rains Hard Man stood a few feet away, saying the sacred words that would bind them in marriage. He was burning a sacred bundle of sage and sweet grass and waved it over them every so often.

Apaniaki's chest heaved upward, and she steadied herself for what she was about to do. She had given up hope of ever seeing Levi again. It had been too long since he'd been staked out. If he had not come yet, then he was surely dead.

She had debated going through with the marriage, for the sake of her child. For a time, she had reasoned, she could suffer through a union with Large Teeth if it meant that her son, for she knew it would be a son, would be taken care of. But the thought of securing the lie with nuptials, and then reinforcing it at Large Teeth's whim turned her stomach. It was not a thing that she could do. She would not betray Levi in such a way. No, today, the band of the people would yet again be looking for a new Chief.

It had been impossible to hide a weapon in her dress as it was all one piece. Made of doeskin, lightened in the sun, and decorated with little red beads all over. So instead, she had hid the blade in her hair. The decorative bone comb that held her long black hair in place, its teeth replaced with a long iron blade made for slashing.

Large Teeth looked at her. His eyes shining brightly. He smiled, and the smile made her want to vomit. She scanned his features then, the wide neck with corded muscles that attached to broad, tanned shoulders. That would be her mark.

As Rains Hard Man finished his last remarks, he asked that they extend their arms to be bound. She did so, and the old man bent to pick up the rawhide cords from his Medicine bag. Apaniaki's other hand cautiously, yet non-chalantly made its way to her hair, where she brushed back a wayward strand, left loose for this very purpose.

Large Teeth's eyes followed her hand, and she batted her eyes at him, mustering a look of love and seduction that she did not know she was capable of. She could see him melt then, and he averted his eyes with a blush. It was then that her hand snapped up the bone handle in her hair, and she lunged at him, her eyes never wavering from their mark—

He caught her wrist, his reflexes panther quick, and she stood there, makeshift knife in hand, fingers un-curling beneath his powerful grip. The knife tumbled from her open hand, and she saw the anger in his eyes. The mad temper.

A gasp went up from the rest of the band, as Large Teeth struck her strongly across the face.

She collapsed to the ground, her head a black maze.

Then someone pointed, and another shouted, "Look."

Large Teeth was ready to strike again, but he stayed his hand. He snapped her up by the wrist with a tight grip, twisting her body awkwardly; so hard she felt her whole arm might snap off.

Three riders had topped the hill behind them, no more than two hundred paces off. This is what had stayed Large Teeth's hand. This is what had caused the others to gasp and point.

She could not believe it, even from this distance she could recognize the figure in the middle. It was him. It was Levi. And the man next to him appeared to be her father. But was he not dead? Was this their ghostly forms, come to visit before continuing to the Sandhills in the east? The third man she could not place.

Large Teeth shoved her away from him then, and she fell to the ground again.

The riders started towards them then, not at a run, a lope, or a trot, but an easy walk. Large Teeth stepped backwards as they came. The others that were gathered around stood dumbfounded.

Then a great murmur went up from the throng, and what they were talking about Apaniaki could not even begin to guess. Could it be that a bride had tried to murder her husband at the altar, or was it about the three riders, and their chief, seemingly risen from the dead.

Then the riders were there, standing no less than ten paces from the crowd. It was indeed Levi, and beside him, her father.

Levi smiled at her, but said nothing. It was that dry smile, as if he was privy to a great joke that no one else in the wide world had ever deciphered. His eyes shifted from her to the knife, to Large Teeth, and still the slight smile did not move from his face.

Large Teeth looked around nervously then, and took two steps backwards, finally breaking free of the place in the ground where his feet had tried to take root, but the crowd had gathered tighter, hemming him in, and obstructing his path of retreat.

Levi slid out of the saddle then, and Apaniaki ran to him, throwing her arms around his neck, her lips searching for his. But Levi averted his face, not allowing his eyes or focus to leave those of Large Teeth, who now stood there dumbly.

She felt his firm hands give her waist a squeeze, a squeeze that spoke so many words, things impossible to speak in one lifetime. He gently moved her out of the way, and towards her father, who beckoned her to him with open arms.

She hugged her father then, melting into him, unable to believe that he was still alive.

With a backwards glance, she saw Levi retrieve two tomahawks from the saddle of the mule he'd ridden in on. Working slowly and easily, he set one on the ground, and from his pocket, he pulled a long ribbon of cloth. Wincing, he took the long cloth and tied a hatchet into his right hand, the one pierced by Large Teeth's arrow. In his other hand he took up the second hatchet, the one he'd laid on the ground.

He turned towards Large Teeth, and the latter stepped forward, peeling off his otter skin shirt in preparation for the fight. Levi tossed the second hatchet onto the ground in front of the man.

Apaniaki started to go to him, to stop him—to stop the madness. But her father held her tighter.

The circle of people widened then, forming a circle. A natural ring for the two to fight. Light Owl and Rains Hard Man, shifted backwards, taking places beside their old friend Black Crow.

LARGE TEETH RETRIEVED THE HATCHET AND tossed it from hand to hand, trying to find its balance, hoping that the action would give wings to his feet and release them of the lead that filled them.

The Napikwan started forward, bearing down on him, hatchet at his side and chest out. He was brash and bullish, advancing on Large Teeth so confidently that the latter felt some of his nerve escape him.

Large Teeth stumbled on his own feet as he attempted to walk backwards, barely catching himself with an outstretched arm. He scrambled up even as the man in front of him continued to approach, continued to press. There was an anger in the man, Large

Teeth could feel it, sense it. It was an anger that bred utter confidence, a confidence that came from a deep knowledge that he was in the right, a knowledge that gave the man complete control over his future. This was the walk of a man that knew the ending, who knew that he would not lose.

The man swung the 'hawk in a wide gleaming arc, and Large Teeth cried out in terror even as he blocked it. The glancing blow caused him to again stumble backwards, and the very edge of the tomahawk having knicked his knuckles, caused them to bleed.

Large Teeth tried to reset, he tried to find space, but still the man came towards him, pressing into his space. Large Teeth swung his own 'hawk wildly, trying to clear a swath around him so he could regain his composure, but the man stopped suddenly, letting Large Teeth's blade swing by him uselessly. Then he continued his forward pressure, the hawk's head now held upright, tense, like a snake before it strikes.

Large Teeth jumped backwards, even as he regretted giving up more ground. The throng behind him parted, letting him retreat further, but still the man came, walking him down.

Large Teeth began to chant, fear coursing through his veins. It was his death song. He found his feet and his courage at last, and rushed forward, swinging wildly at the man before him, but even as he did so, he saw the man take a stutter step back.

There was a crack, and he felt the hatchet leave his grip, followed by a sudden flash of searing pain. Large Teeth looked down at his hand. The pain caused him to momentarily be outside of himself. His wrist was broken and bleeding. He could see the white of his own bone, and his hand hung uselessly still connected to his arm by a thin rope of flesh.

It was as if he was looking at the hand of another.

Large Teeth stood weaponless now, his tomahawk laying some way off.

The man gave a vicious kick to the inside of his knee—another crunch—Large Teeth fell.

The Napikwan swung a heavy fist that dropped Large Teeth to all fours. His head a blur, and copper in his mouth. He had stones in his mouth—his teeth.

The man picked him up, grasping him by his neck, and with weak hands Large Teeth tried to grasp the arms that held him. The man swung him backwards, as if he had just picked up a stray yellow dog, weakened with age, and light with starvation. He slammed Large Teeth onto the ground, driving breath from his body, and shaking his bones so thoroughly, that he heard, as well as felt, his ribs crack.

The hits came hard and fast then, and just before the blackness took him, they stopped.

The man had stood up. He hovered above Large Teeth. He had not killed him. The fool. Large Teeth's terror returned then, not at being killed, but at having to live. At being exiled from the tribe, at having to live off the scraps of others, at the insults they would spit at him. He struggled to his knees, watching the Long Knife walk away from him, and then he felt the smooth handle of a knife as it was pressed into his good hand.

He glanced up, and Steals Many Horses nodded to him.

He rose to his feet then, his heart pounding, blood running into his eyes. He wiped them. His breath was ragged, but he had a singular purpose now—plunge the knife into the Napikwan's back.

He stumbled forward, his legs gathering speed, somewhat surprised that he was still capable of moving them. His knee was on fire. Still the man walked away from him, seemingly oblivious to the danger. Large Teeth raised the knife in preparation for a hard downward thrust, maybe the last of his life, when he heard the snap of a bowstring and felt something hit him. It felt like he'd been hit with a rock. Like a young boy had thrown a rock and struck him hard in the chest.

The pain came next though. A searing pain that again dropped him to a position of worship. He looked down to see the shaft of an arrow protruding from his chest. He saw the feather then, a dirty white and black plume, a goose feather, made up of a hundred individual strands all moving under the weight of the warm spring breeze. The markings on the end of the arrow belonged to Black Crow. He saw the nock then, the small etchings where the wood had been expertly shaped by a sharp knife. He saw it all in tiny detail, even as he tumbled sideways.

His vision narrowed. His eyes focused on the scene that lay just beyond the end of the arrow's shaft. He saw the man, his arms around Apaniaki, drawing her in for a kiss, saying something to her. Then they were blocked from view by a leathern foot. The threadwork zigging and zagging across the seam that held the upper portion of the moccasin to the sole of the boot.

His eyes lolled upward, climbing the figure that stood above him. It was Black Crow, who stood, another arrow nocked, its black obsidian tip catching the brilliant rays of the sun.

"You lived like a dog, now you may die as one."

Then he heard the twang, and flinched at the pressure that pierced his heart. Night descended on him then, and he heard screams in the blackness of it. He heard a coyote yap some way off, and then its family answered with low cackles.

⸙

LEVI TOOK APANIAKI IN HIS ARMS. NOW when she pressed her lips to his, he drank them like water, long and deep, as if it was the last time he would ever drink. He pulled her closer, feeling her body against his.

"You're mine," Levi said. "Damn if anyone else was going to touch you."

The End

A NOTE FROM THE AUTHOR

Thank YOU for reading. It is because of you that I can do this.

Indie books don't come with big traditional marketing budgets. We rely on word of mouth. One of the best ways to help me write more of the types of books you like, is to leave a review.

If you enjoyed this book or even if you hated it, please leave a review.

STAY IN TOUCH

Author Updates, Short Stories, Essays and more!

Never miss a new release.

Join today at frankkiddauthor.com

ABOUT THE AUTHOR

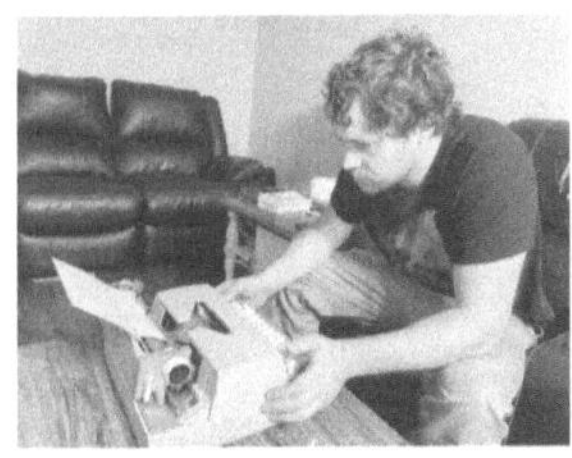

Frank Kidd is an American author and screenwriter living in Missouri. He writes across genres, but specializes in westerns and historical adventure. He is also a veteran, an outdoorsman, and an amateur historian. Some of his favorite authors include Louis L'Amour, Jack London, Richard Matheson, and Robert E. Howard. You can follow his work via his online publication, Pulp West, or on his website.

www.ingramcontent.com/pod-product-compliance
Lightning Source LLC
LaVergne TN
LVHW041924090826
845145LV00015B/575

* 9 7 8 1 9 6 6 8 4 7 0 1 4 *